NO CHOICE BUT MURDER

An absolutely gripping murder mystery full of twists

NORMAN RUSSELL

An Oldminster Mystery Book 4

D1251561

Joffe Books, London
www.joffebooks.com

First published in Great Britain in 2022

Cover art by Dee Dee Book Covers

ISBN: 978-1-80405-546-5

1. HUSBANDS AND WIVES

'Ladies and gentlemen, I give you a toast: Mr Louis Gillette and the Rembrandt Gallery!'

Councillor Jimmy Parle, the Deputy Lord Mayor of Oldminster, managed to inject some life into his words, which concluded a decidedly lacklustre speech. Jimmy Parle knew nothing about Art-with-a-capital-A, but the Lord Mayor, Edward Billington, had accosted him on the Friday of the previous week, and had told him that he flatly refused to go to the reception, which was to be held at the gallery's premises in King's Arcade.

'Chichester City are playing at home on Tuesday and I'm not missing that game for a couple of glasses of plonk and a cardboard plate of canapés. So you go, Jimmy, we've got to show willing. I'll go next year.'

'If there *is* a next year,' muttered Jimmy, looking out of the window of the Lord Mayor's parlour at the green roof of the municipal baths beyond the Town Hall car park.

'Why, what do you mean?' asked the Lord Mayor sharply. 'What have you heard?'

'Nothing,' said Jimmy Parle. 'But there's a big Bond Street jeweller wanting to open in the Arcade, and nobody's shifting. They'd love to open in Louis Gillette's premises. And anyway . . .'

Jimmy crossed the room and whispered in the Lord Mayor's ear.

'What! Near bankrupt?' said Billington. 'I don't believe it. He's got that millionaire father-in-law to back him up whenever he needs a cash injection. You get out to the Rembrandt Gallery next Tuesday, and do some glad-handing, and a bit of chatting up. Smiles all round. It doesn't matter what you say: nobody will be listening. All the guests will just want to drain the place dry and get on home.'

'Maybe they'll buy some of the paintings,' said Jimmy with a smile.

'Maybe they will. And maybe pigs will fly. My Rhoda likes seascapes — well, you've seen that lovely painting hanging in the hall of our house. Lovely, it is. You can see all the little curly waves, and a little red lighthouse standing on a cliff. You'll see nothing like that at the Rembrandt.'

'Bishop Poindexter went last year.'

'Yes, he did. But his engagement book's full all next Tuesday.'

Ted Billington was a burly, red-faced man, owner of a chain of butchers' shops in Oldminster and some of the villages lying about the old cathedral town. Jimmy Parle could have been his twin. Equally bulbous-nosed and red-faced, he and the Lord Mayor were known locally as Tweedledum and Tweedledee. Jimmy was in the dry-cleaning business.

'How did you know that the bishop was fully booked for Tuesday?'

The Lord Mayor gave a full-throated laugh. 'He's got a season ticket to City. He's going to the match with me, in my car. Enjoy yourself on Tuesday. And don't buy anything!'

* * *

Chloe McArthur, champagne flute in one hand and balancing a paper plate of petits-fours in the other, moved through the crowded rooms of the Rembrandt Gallery, which occupied a prime spot in the King's Arcade. Opened in 1905, the Arcade was a charming art nouveau affair, and it was considered to be the crowning glory of Oldminster High Street.

Louis Gillette's choice of paintings, a rather amorphous collection of washed-out watercolours, sloppy oils and strident acrylics, were not much to her taste — she liked clear, simple lines, without the distraction of fussy adornment. A slim, handsome woman in her forties, never seen without a jacquard silk scarf to set off her jacket and skirt combinations, she wore her short fair hair in a style which swept over her brow and accentuated her grey eyes.

No, it wasn't the art that had drawn Chloe to the opening; for her, the more interesting exhibits were the host and his guests.

Her work as a private detective had long trained her to produce quick mental sketches of people in crowded rooms. It was that ability that had once caused her to realise that a mild, inoffensive clergyman at a jewellery auction was in fact a notorious robber: his bearing was all wrong, and his hands were too restless; and once she'd done a double take, she'd recognised his face from the police circulars. She had quietly whispered in his ear, and he had beaten a hasty retreat. She and her business partner, Noel Greenspan, had been stalking more dangerous prey that day than the potential jewel thief.

And now she looked at Louis Gillette, who had just acknowledged the Deputy Lord Mayor's bland platitudes with a modest thank-you speech, and was talking animatedly to a lady wearing a mauve kaftan and a rather daring turban of peacock blue. The gallery owner was a man in his fifties, tall and slim, with a fine head of carefully nurtured grey hair. He was one of those men who always appear to be tanned, even in the depth of an English winter. He was wearing a well-cut suit of oatmeal tweed, enlivened by a dashing scarlet handkerchief in the top pocket of the jacket. But Chloe's observant eye saw the man's fingernails were bitten to the quick, and the sharp angle of his jaw where he was quite unconsciously grinding his teeth. What was the matter with him? She knew him quite well, because his wife Lydia — svelte, ash-blonde Lydia — was by way of being one of her friends, a long-term member of the Cathedral Ladies' Guild. She was not there that evening.

She spotted Caleb Brewster, an elderly man dressed rather unfetchingly in a baggy grey suit; he beckoned her over to where he was standing in front of an oil painting of a cardboard box with one side torn away and lying on an orange ground. It was by someone called Eric Pistol, and was called *Is this all there is?*.

'He wants one-hundred-and-seventy-five pounds for it,' said Caleb. 'How are you, Chloe? When are you going to marry that boss of yours?'

'Noel hasn't been my boss for years,' Chloe told him gently. 'I'm a partner in the firm. Greenspan *and* McArthur. Remember?' He looked a bit embarrassed at his mistake, so she saved his feelings by adding, 'How are you, Mr Brewster? Enjoying your retirement? But you actually liked teaching teenagers, didn't you?'

'I did. It was marvellous, not to put too fine a point on it. Fun. Treat them right, and they'll treat *you* right. But these paintings . . . The trouble with Louis Gillette is that he has no taste in art at all. It's tragic, really. Everything here is third-rate, and nobody's going to buy any of it. He's wasting a lot of money on feeding and watering us this evening. You see that woman he's talking to? She's here for a spot of self-advertisement. She's been handing out cards for her shop for mystics in Chichester. Reading chakras, crystal gazing, tarot cards, that sort of thing. She's no interest in poor Louis's frightful exhibition.'

'He still contrives to make a living, though,' Chloe ventured. 'I bought a nice little oil painting from him about five years ago. It was an original.'

'Well, yes,' said Mr Brewster. 'He had a bit of financial acumen in those days. But he knows that his father-in-law will bail him out if he gets into trouble, so he can persist in that stubborn illusion of his that he is a man of taste. He isn't. Look at that suit! Well, there's nothing wrong with the suit, but it's wrong for *him*. And as for his father-in-law bailing him out — well, I've heard rumours that Simon Bolt is going to tighten the purse strings. What Louis Gillette should do is turn this place into a sort of artists' collective shop — a workshop for art classes and children's groups, a small gallery space and a counter to sell locally made pottery and paintings — there's nothing like that at the moment in Oldminster. He should make a bonfire of all this rubbish and start to provide his clients with a genuine service. Maybe he could go into partnership with that lady in the turban.'

'Who told you that Simon Bolt was going to tighten the purse strings?'

'It was Brooke Cliveden, my chiropodist, who has that marvellous Aladdin's cave of a surgery in the shops at the Triangle.'

'Brooke Cliveden? He's my chiropodist, too.'

'Is he, really? I didn't think you'd need Brooke's services. You're so, so — well, *you* know. He's very knowledgeable on the doings of Oldminster's Jewish community, but in fact there's not much that he doesn't hear about. He literally sits at the feet of many of the great and the good, including Sister Maureen of the Daughters of Charity, and Bishop Poindexter's sister, Lady Maine.'

Caleb took another swig of champagne, then realised his glass was empty and glanced around for more, but the free drinks seemed to be at an end. 'I'm off, Chloe,' he said. 'Off to watch telly. That champagne wasn't bad at all, I'll give him that. He's not mean, is our Louis. But if Brooke Cliveden is right, then he'll have to be tightening his belt soon.'

When he had gone, Chloe McArthur wandered through the rooms, noting that most of the guests were not looking at the pictures, but talking to each other. It was nearing nine, and she couldn't spot any sold stickers on any of the meretricious offerings of the Rembrandt Gallery. Caleb Brewster was right. Poor Louis Gillette had been in the wrong business for years.

Louis had managed to get rid of the flamboyant mystic and was listening to a young man dressed very respectably in a charcoal grey suit with white shirt and dark blue tie. Chloe noted that Louis could not meet the young man's eye, as though he was either frightened or ashamed. She edged nearer to hear what the young man was saying.

'There's no question of coercion, Mr Gillette, and I resent your even suggesting it. But three months is too long, and next week we intend to take action.'

That, thought Chloe, sounded very much like a demand for money — rent arrears, perhaps? Poor Louis Gillette! This was not going to be one of his more successful evenings.

A mobile in Louis Gillette's pocket set up a busy vibration, and the young man moved away. Louis walked into an alcove near the fireplace. Chloe stood quite still, unwilling to reveal that she was only inches away from her host. He listened in silence for a while, and she could hear the sound of a man's voice coming from the phone. Then, quite clearly, she heard Louis Gillette say, 'What! No choice but murder? You actually heard him say that? Well, he must have changed his mind since then. As a matter of fact, he's written me a very nice letter . . . Yes, but thank you anyway for the warning.'

At ten o'clock the party broke up, and the guests began to drift out into the High Street. Louis Gillette was standing in the middle of one of the empty rooms, apparently lost in thought. Natural compulsion made her go over to him.

'Is everything all right, Louis?' she asked. 'You look distracted—'

'All right?' cried Louis, with a loud, liberating laugh. 'Everything's fine! Why shouldn't it be? Was it Browning who wrote: "God's in his heaven, all's right with the world"? Well, Chloe, that's how I feel tonight. Now, I must lock the place up and go home before Lydia gets back.'

'Where is Lydia tonight?' Chloe asked, a little unnerved by Louis's fixed smile.

'She goes to an embroidery class on Tuesday evenings. She appreciates your friendship, Chloe. She's fragile in so many ways and needs an understanding friend.'

Louis Gillette was proving to be an enigma, Chloe thought, as she left him sorting through his keys. That burst of laughter had been real enough, but the gallery owner had been quite unable to hide from his eyes the look of some nagging anxiety that revealed a more believable aspect of the man within.

* * *

The ancient cathedral city of Oldminster was large enough to be a real urban hub, a vibrant working town, its streets lined with small shops, especially in the old quarter to the west of Cathedral Green, where the majestic cathedral of St Peter rose on its mound. The High Street, celebrated for the King's Arcade, also offered Marks and Spencer, with its enticing food hall, together with branches of other popular retail outlets. To the south, in what had been a fallow area of ruined meadows, a branch of Sainsbury's had recently opened.

On the far side of Sainsbury's car park, on what was called 'the wrong side' of the River Ashe, stood a block of utilitarian 1960s flats, and in one of these flats lived Jack Prosser, who was regarding himself in the mirror above the fireplace of his living room, while his girlfriend tidied herself up in the bathroom.

What did the mirror show him? A good-looking man in his early fifties who took care of himself, still athletic and a marathon runner, head of PE at Oldminster High School. He'd had his share of relationships, but had never forgotten his childhood friend, who had been wooed and won by someone who wasn't deserving of her. He'd watched the two of them — her and her husband — over three decades, pretending to console himself with the fact that nothing could be changed. But whenever he began a relationship with another woman, *her* image would come into his mind, and the affair would peter out.

He looked out of the window. It was just after nine, and quite dark, though Sainsbury's was a blaze of light. White headlights and red taillights flashed and gleamed in the vast car park.

She came out of the bathroom and retrieved her bag and coat from the bedroom. She looked no different to him now than she had looked in the early eighties, when they had danced and dreamed, and listened to Prince's 'When Doves Cry' and Michael Jackson's 'Billie Jean'. They were all gone, now, lost with the ashes of their dreams.

While he personally felt no guilt at all, he knew that she agonised about her adultery — an old-fashioned word that hadn't yet lost its baleful force. They kissed in his cramped little hallway, and once again she was unable to meet his steady gaze. Something would have to be done, something drastic. It was time to concoct a plan.

* * *

Lydia Gillette stumbled across Sainsbury's car park, key in hand, ready to make her own car greet her from the dark with its flashing taillights. Oh God! How soiled and ashamed she felt! Louis had long since abdicated his physical duties as a husband, and Jack, her childhood friend, the man whom she should have married, made her feel like a real woman again. But among all the optimistic pleasure, there would always be the searing pain of guilt. What was to become of her?

* * *

'How did it go?'

'Very well, Lydia. A great deal of interest was shown, as I'd anticipated.'

The Gillettes lived in a quiet, settled suburban road to the north of the cathedral. Their house was a large, detached residence, built in the 1880s of yellow brick, with various stone Gothic flourishes. It stood in decent, manageable gardens. The rooms were light and airy, but cold and lifeless. Upstairs there was a room to the rear of the house with bars fitted to the windows. It had been a nursery in Victorian times, when the lady of the house expected to have children as a matter of course, a family to nurture and love. She and Louis had not been able to have children.

'Yes, very successful. I think things are about to turn a corner. Drink, my dear?'

'A gin and tonic would be nice, though it's a bit late for indulging.'

My dear . . .

They sat together in the drawing room, he in his oatmeal suit, which matched the oatmeal carpets and the oatmeal sofas. She had to admit to herself that Louis was singularly lacking in taste. Despite his profession, he had no taste in art, no taste in furnishings, no taste in clothes. Jack Prosser's flat was full of colour and personality. It looked like a place that had been lived in. This house of theirs in Gladstone Road had all the intimacy of a squat.

'How was the embroidery?'

'Oh . . . Fine.'

'It's not all vestments, is it? Stoles, and chasubles, Catholic stuff?'

'Oh, no. There's all kinds of things.'

What business is it of yours, anyway? You're not really interested. Just as well, perhaps.

'Well, I'm off to bed. Don't be too long, my dear.'

My dear . . .

* * *

A few miles to the north of Oldminster lay Grace Hall, a rambling Tudor mansion that had the distinction of being converted from a shabby country-house hotel to a private dwelling, contrary to the usual run of things in the twenty-first century. In the main house, which had been skilfully restored to create a comfortable but fascinating home, with a great hall, dim old Tudor parlours, and en-suite bedrooms, lived Manfred Tauber and his second wife, Corinne.

Tauber had the bearing of a country squire, and took the calling seriously — meting out succour, justice and rewards within his little domain as and when required. He was a heavily built man, in his seventies, with grey hair turning silver, a man with a gentle, beautifully articulated voice which made quite ordinary observations sound like poetry, or mannered prose.

On the sunny afternoon of Friday, 14 September, Manfred Tauber sat in the massive library of Grace Hall, a library artfully contrived from what had been the long gallery of the ancient house. Its ranks of shelves held Tauber's celebrated collection of rare books, a collection which attracted certain rich bibliophiles who would accept his price for a treasured volume without demur. He would have shuddered to be labelled a bookseller. No, he was a connoisseur, and so were the select men and women who came to stay there a day or so, browsing his collection.

But on that Friday, he was giving his whole attention to his wife. Corinne Tauber was not yet forty, and was a very beautiful woman, openly admired by her husband, who enjoyed indulging her every whim, and showing her off proudly to his friends. She had expensive tastes, but then, so had he.

'Where will you stay in town, darling?' asked Manfred Tauber. 'You didn't like it at Claridge's last month. Too noisy, you said.'

'Well, there were an awful lot of foreigners there that week, and they do talk so loudly all the time, and in their own languages, so that nobody knows what they're talking about. So, I thought I'd stay at the Connaught this time. Poppy St Leger stayed there last week, and said it was marvellous.'

'That diamond ring you saw at Asprey's — why don't you buy it this time, sweetie? I don't like you doing without things.'

Corinne was dressed with exquisite taste, her whole wardrobe modelled on that of the Duchess of Cambridge. She wore good clothes well and had been a very successful model until she had met Manfred. They had suited each other admirably. He acquired a beautiful, elegant wife, and she had got herself a fabulously rich husband. She crossed the room from where she had been appraising herself in a dim old mirror above the Tudor fireplace and planted a light kiss on the top of her husband's head. As she drew away from him, he saw the look of quiet affection that she gave him. 'She married him for his money,' people said. Well, they were wrong — money was only part of the bargain. She was off now for a week's shopping in London. Once there, she knew that he had given her carte blanche to do whatever she liked.

'Mr Tauber?' A cultured voice interrupted his thoughts. 'A Mr Charles Deacon is asking to see you.'

Manfred Tauber kept a full staff at Grace Hall, including a house manager — what they had called a butler, in the old days. Williams was not the stereotypical stately figure — he was a young man, who favoured a black lounge suit, but he was more than master of the great mansion. After that of Tauber, Williams' word was law.

'Deacon? Oh, yes, I remember him. He was a counter clerk in that little bank I owned — the one I sold out to NatWest. But that was a few years ago. Show him in, will you?'

Tauber had seen many men of Deacon's kind, men who had gone to seed and let themselves go, men who couldn't rise to the challenges of everyday life, fell ill — or their wives fell ill — and then found themselves penniless. So it was with Deacon. A sick wife, a dead-end job from which he'd been dismissed for poor timekeeping. Arrears of rent . . .

He raised a hand to quell the wretched narrative of failure, and Deacon stopped speaking. He sat in a chair near the fireplace, the picture of defeat.

'What figure are we talking about, Deacon?' asked Tauber.

'Well, sir, there's £340 rent arrears, and then—'

'Never mind the details, man! Just tell me the sum total of your debts.'

The voice came small and low, the voice of a man too ashamed to look Tauber in the face. 'Three thousand pounds.'

Manfred Tauber rose from his chair and sat at a bureau near the window. After a minute, he rose, and handed Deacon a cheque. The man looked at it and cried aloud in joy.

'Oh, Mr Tauber, sir, I never thought you'd be so generous! How can I repay you? You've brought me back to life.'

'Well, well, we're poor mortals if we can't help each other. No, don't say anything else, there's a good chap. But leave your address with Williams. I'd like to keep in touch.'

He could hear the man's sobs as Williams showed him to the door.

* * *

Williams saw Deacon to the gate. On his way back to the house he fell in with a grim, shaven-headed man with tattoos on his neck, who had emerged from a path leading out of a spinney which housed some garden sheds. He was carrying an axe and was dressed in the indeterminate dull clothes of a gardener.

'Another beggar, was it, John?' the man growled. 'Another bloody parasite? How much did he give him?'

'Three thousand pounds, Danny.'

'Three thousand!' Danny O'Toole snorted in disgust. 'Mr Tauber's too kind for his own good. All those old books, all that fancy antique furniture — he's going soft. He needs to watch out, and so do we.'

Williams found Manfred Tauber in his office, a very modern, no-frills suite of rooms in the rear portion of the ground floor. He stood at the door, regarding his employer as he tapped away rapidly at the keyboard of a computer. Without turning to look at Williams, he said, 'There's still a very steady market for gilts, if you know the right places to look.'

'Danny thinks you're going soft,' said Williams. 'He thinks you should watch your step.'

Tauber swung round from his computer.

'Does he really? Well, I'm just glad he cares! I'll certainly watch my step, Williams — I've been doing that for a long time, now, if the truth be known. Danny O'Toole's a good sort, but he's not always right in his judgements. Things are going very well at the moment. Very well indeed. Next week should clear the air.'

* * *

'Jack? It's me. I'm worried about Louis. It's after nine, and he's still not back from the gallery. He's almost always home early on Friday evenings. I've rung and rung, but there's no answer, either from his office phone or his mobile.'

'Do you want me to go round there, Lydia?'

'Would you? There's a night security guard at the Arcade, but he can only be contacted by mobile, and I don't know his number.'

Jack Prosser was about to say, 'Don't worry,' but it would have been the wrong thing to say. Louis Gillette, he knew, was a creature of habit, and if he'd not answered his office phone, then something was possibly wrong. Could this be the opportunity he'd been waiting for? A time to be alone with his rival?

It took him fifteen minutes to drive back into town in his Fiesta, and he was able to park near the gallery. The High Street was still thronging with people, some having finished their weekend's shopping, others on their way to theatres, cinemas or nightclubs. Why had he thought the town would be deserted? After all, it wasn't yet half past nine.

He rang the bell beside the closed Arcade gates, and in a few moments the security man appeared, and looked at him through the closed gates. He was in his thirties, and dressed rather like a police officer, complete with crackling radio and peaked cap. There were a lot of men like this these days, he thought, policemen in all but name and authority.

'Mr Gillette? Yes, he's still here. You can see the lights are on in the gallery. I expect he'll be closing up soon. He stays late now and then. I'll let you in, but I'll have to lock up behind you, if you don't mind. I'll be in my office at the far end when you want to be let out.'

The man unlocked the gates, stood aside to let Jack enter, and then hurried away, his footsteps echoing in the empty Arcade, which was dimly illuminated by small LED lights set beneath the glazed arc of the roof, emergency lighting to deter robbers during the dark hours of the night. Lydia was getting too jumpy about her husband — it was partly the wretched guilt that she felt over her being unfaithful — but it was odd that Louis had not phoned to say that he would be late.

The front door of the Rembrandt Gallery was closed but unlocked. The premises were fully lit, the walls still hung with the paintings from the previous Tuesday's exhibition. The place seemed to be embraced by an uncanny silence. This was the night when he could be rid of Louis Gillette for good . . .

He opened the door and stepped into the gallery.

2. STILL LIFE WITH BRONZE

When the call had come from Jubilee House, the head-quarters of the Oldshire Constabulary, Detective Sergeant Glyn Edwards left his wife Sandra preparing for bed. 'I'm sorry about this, love,' he'd said, and she had given him that amused smile of acceptance of their joint lot that he had come to value so much.

DS Edwards drove into town in his Ford Fiesta and found that part of the High Street adjoining the King's Arcade already had a couple of police cars parked alongside, their lights flashing, and he could see a couple of uniformed constables guarding the entrance. The uniforms at Central had evidently had a quiet night. They were all part of the panoply of concern attending a burglary and a sudden death.

He sat in his car for a few minutes, dragging on a cigarette. Sandra wanted him to give up smoking, said it would hurt their chances of adopting a child. But he only smoked a couple of cigarettes a day. Well five, maybe . . . He regarded himself ruefully in the rear mirror. He was only thirty-eight, but he looked older, gaunt and hatchet-faced. He'd give it up and start going to the gym again.

As he left the car, he was approached by one of the two constables guarding the door, a woman in her early twenties, bright-eyed and eager. Her air of constrained excitement suggested that this was her first burglary. She introduced herself as PC Anita Crane.

'SOCO are already here,' she went on, 'and the medical examiner — a Dr Dunwoody.'

'Good. I know him well. We'll go in there, presently, Constable, and while SOCO finish their work, you and I will make our own assessment. Did you take a statement from the person who discovered the body? I'll need to speak to them first.'

The constable flicked over the pages of her notebook.

'He's a Mr Jack Prosser, sir, and he lives in number eight Bankside Flats, just by Sainsbury's. He said that he was a friend of Mr Gillette's wife, who'd phoned him to say that she was worried, as her husband hadn't come home, and it was getting late.'

'That's interesting. I wonder why she didn't come herself to look for her husband. Where is he now, this Jack Prosser?'

'He's sitting in that late-night Chinese takeaway across the street — the Golden Gate. He wouldn't stay in the Arcade, sir, got very agitated when I suggested that he could wait in the security man's office until you arrived. I made it clear that he would need to be questioned by a detective before he could go home.'

'Kicked up a fuss, did he?'

'Not a fuss, sir, but he was shaking and sweating. I suppose he'd never seen a dead body before.'

'Hm . . . How old are you, PC Crane?'

'Twenty-three, sir.'

'Have you seen many dead bodies before? No. And did you go all of a tremble when you saw Mr Gillette lying dead?'

'I was upset, of course, but I was on the job, sir. No time for personal feelings. Do you think—'

'I don't think anything yet, PC Crane. But it's a point worth noting. Let's go and see this Jack Prosser now, in the Golden Gate, before he gets itchy feet.'

The welcome smell of Chinese food hit their noses as they made their way into the warmth of the Golden Gate. There were a number of tables covered with chequered red-and-white cloths, each with its own condiment set and menu card. The walls were covered in black and silver wallpaper, with a pattern of writhing dragons. At the far end of the shop was a counter.

The premises were closed and sitting at one of the tables were two men. Glyn knew Jimmy Yip, the proprietor, who got up from the table and shook hands with him. Glyn looked at the other man sitting at the table, cradling a cup of tea in his hands. So this was Jack Prosser, who had kicked up such a fuss about staying in the Arcade. Early fifties, handsome, good physical shape. It was very obvious that he was badly shaken. Jimmy Yip left the two men together, and DS Edwards sat down at the table. PC Crane stood some way apart, guarding the door from the street. Glyn showed Jack Prosser his warrant card.

'Mr Prosser,' he said, 'will you tell me how you came to visit the King's Arcade tonight?'

'I made a statement to that police constable—'

'Yes, I know you did, but now I want you to tell *me*.'

'I'm an old friend of Louis Gillette's wife, Lydia. She rang me tonight about nine fifteen to say that Louis hadn't come home from the gallery, and would I go to see if he was all right.'

'Was it usual for her to ask you to check on Mr Gillette?'

'What? No, this was the first time.'

'And were you a friend of Mr Gillette, too?'

'Yes. Why, what do you mean? Of course I was his friend. But I've known Lydia for years, before ever she was married.'

'Did she say why she didn't go to find her husband herself?'

He shook his head. 'Perhaps she didn't feel it looked quite right, or perhaps she didn't like to come into the gallery at night. Lydia's quite . . . timid isn't the wrong word, but she's been protected all her life, you understand. Things that seem quite ordinary to most people are a little frightening for her.'

'So what did you do?'

'I came here by car from Bankside and parked near the gallery. I rang the bell, and the night watchman let me in. I went down to the gallery, and found the door open — I told the constable all this.'

'Bear with me, Mr Prosser. A few more questions and you'll be free to go. Tell me briefly what you saw.'

'The gallery was a blaze of light but seemed to be empty. I went through the gallery and into the back room — I'd been in there on other occasions, you understand. I saw . . . I saw Louis Gillette lying dead across the table. It was horrible.'

Prosser turned deadly pale. Glyn wondered whether he was going to faint.

'Did you touch the body?'

'No, I didn't go near it! I ran out into the Arcade and shouted for the security man.'

'You told the nightwatchman that Mr Gillette had been murdered. What made you say that?'

'I . . .' Prosser stumbled and stopped. 'Did I say that?'

Glyn waited. Sometimes it was better to be silent, let the witness talk. Had Louis spotted something wrong with the scene, or was there something else on his mind?

'Well, wasn't he murdered?' Prosser said, still nonplussed. 'The safe was open and there was a statue on the floor looking as if it had been used to knock him down — I thought he'd been tortured for the combination or something.' He looked as if he was about to say something else but didn't.

'Thank you, Mr Prosser,' Glyn said after an uncomfortable silence didn't yield anything more. 'We'll need you to come into Jubilee House tomorrow to make a written statement. What is your occupation, may I ask?'

'I'm head of PE at Oldminster High School. Can I go now? It's very late.'

At Glyn's nod, PC Crane opened the shop door, and Jack Prosser hurried away.

'What d'you think, Constable?'

'I think — I think he was terrified of you, Sergeant. It was as though he knew something terrible, and that any moment you were going to ask him about it.'

'Yes, he was frightened of me, wasn't he? He could hardly keep his voice straight.' Glyn felt suddenly impatient to get to the crime scene, but as he stood, he added, 'You have an advantage over me, Constable. You've seen the crime scene and I haven't. Did you notice anything else about Jack Prosser's statement that didn't seem right?'

'Well, sir, something was a bit off.' She narrowed her eyes and thought for a moment, and then a smile spread across her face. 'He said he didn't approach the body, sir.'

'But . . . ?'

'But there's no way he could have seen the safe was open from the doorway — he would have had to walk right up to Louis Gillette's body to spot that!'

* * *

PC Crane seemed so eager to revisit the crime scene that Glyn wondered whether she was going to drag him into the Arcade by the sleeve. But once over the threshold, he made the young woman stand still beside him. A large banner, stretching across the Arcade high above them, carried the message: KING'S ARCADE AUTUMN EVENT.

'The trick to detective work, PC Crane, is looking at everything carefully — seeing something familiar with fresh eyes. Why not give it a try? Tell me what you see.'

PC Crane frowned out at the shopfronts. 'Well, sir, it's hard to see the King's Arcade with fresh eyes — I've known it since I was a nipper — but I'll try. There are ten shops on each side, and at the far end is the Arcade office and the public toilets.'

'Let's look in more detail at the shops. I know you're raring to go, Constable, but while you're with me, you've got to think like a detective: slow and steady. So, tell me about the shops.'

'On the left-hand side, sir, we start with Polly Atkins, a teen dress shop. Next—'

'Hang on! Is it open or closed? Lights on, or dark?'

'It's dark and closed. Next to that there's Moore's the stationers, likewise dark and closed. Then comes a fancy French cake shop. Dark and closed. Then we come to the bag shop, where you can get a tote bag for £300, so my girlfriend tells me. They've got security lighting on. The next one up, number five, is empty. Number six is Your Choice Computers, and number seven is an optician's, both dark and closed.

'And finally, we come to the Rembrandt Gallery, which is three shops knocked into one, entered from the door of number eight. The doors to nine and ten were converted to windows years ago. As you can see, sir, the premises are a blaze of light.'

Glyn Edwards wondered whether he'd detected a hint of sarcasm there, but a glance at PC Crane showed him the young woman was evidently enjoying her brief stint as a detective. She had a ludicrously fresh complexion, and bright round blue eyes. Police officers seemed to be getting younger every day.

'Before we continue our exercise, Constable, let me just ask you a couple of questions. When you entered the premises, was there a notice on the gallery door — the door of number eight — saying whether it was open or closed?'

PC Crane screwed up her eyes in concentration.

'Yes, sir. There was a card hanging behind the door, and it read *CLOSED*.'

'I see. And when you saw the body what was your first conclusion? What kind of a crime did you think had been committed?'

'Well, sir, it looked to me like a breaking and entering gone wrong. The perpetrator fled the scene.'

'Was the front door locked?'

'No, sir, it was closed, but not locked.'

'So, your villain hardly fled from the scene, as he took time to close the door behind him. Now, tell me about the other shops, starting with this one opposite Polly Atkins.'

'That's number twenty, sir, which is a fabric shop. Closed, but with security lighting on. Then we have Estelle's Perfumery, a fancy scent shop, closed and dark. Number eighteen is Fox's Bookshop, closed and dark. Number seventeen's empty. Then we have a tailors and a women's fashion outlet, both dark and closed. Number fourteen is Troxler's Swiss Café, then All Things Photographic, closed but with security lighting and window grilles. Then we have an empty shop to let, and finally Stoddard's the jewellers, closed, with security grilles down, and full lighting on.'

'Excellent. Can you see where all this is leading?'

'No, sir. At least—'

'Exactly. If I were a burglar, I'd make a beeline for a jeweller's shop with empty premises beside it. I tell you now, Constable, grille or no grille, I could get into that shop in less than half an hour from the safety of that empty shop next door. I could cram my pockets with jewels, and watches, and necklaces — but if I were to rob an art gallery, I could hardly hide a painting under my coat! So I think that our burglar probably had a private reason for choosing this particular shop to rob. And I've deduced all that just by standing here!'

The constable laughed.

'Wow! I've learnt a lot this evening, sir. Shall we go and view the scene of the crime? SOCO should be finished by now.'

'Well, there's just one more thing we haven't spoken about: CCTV.' Glyn pointed at a camera facing the gallery. 'One of our most invaluable tools. We should be able to get something from the nightwatchman when we speak to him. What shift are you working, Constable?'

'Ten to seven, sir.'

'Good. Well, you keep with me, PC Crane, and we'll look into the crime together. Lead on!'

* * *

Sergeant Glyn Edwards stood on the threshold of Louis Gillette's inner office, the third of the knocked-together shops, watching the scene-of-crime team finishing their business. He made no attempt to engage the white-suited figures in conversation, but silently acknowledged a nodded greeting from the senior officer by raising a hand.

He was content to wait for SOCO to finish their gathering of evidence. They were skilled and dedicated gatherers of information at a crime scene, careful not to contaminate evidence, and presenting the detectives with an invaluable dossier of information to support their own investigations.

He regarded the crime scene.

Lying across a desk was the body of a man in his fifties, a slender figure, with a fine head of carefully nurtured grey hair. He was wearing a suit of oatmeal tweed. The dead man's arms were sprawled out at an odd angle across the desk, and even from where he stood Glyn Edwards could see that his nails were badly bitten. The man's eyes were still open, and his face was suffused with a cherry red colour. Glyn stooped down over the body, and smelt what might have been peaches, and alcohol, near to the mouth.

Sitting near the desk on an upright chair was Dr Raymond Dunwoody, the duty medical examiner, a man nearing sixty, with thinning grey hair and long, delicate fingers. He caught Glyn's eye, but before he could speak a tall, broad-shouldered woman in her fifties with the pale complexion of a redhead appeared by his side.

'DS Edwards, isn't it?' she said. 'Jen Wilberforce — I'm the SOCO team leader. We met last year, when we investigated that bacon slicer business. Well, Sergeant, there's something very odd about this sudden death. It looks like a burglary gone wrong, because the safe's open, and everything's taken from it. And that bronze statue of Apollo has been knocked over or thrown down — there it is, in that evidence bag. Owner tackles burglar, perhaps with that statue, burglar gets away, flees the premises — meanwhile the owner here has a heart attack after the shock?'

Glyn frowned at her, puzzled. 'Odd kind of burglary, isn't it? I thought people generally stole art from galleries, rather than going for papers in the safe. It's not like art galleries deal in cash only — what are the chances of actual money being in the safe on any given day?' He waved his hand around at the paintings that had hung on the wall all week. 'I mean, they're not to my taste, but surely . . . ?'

'All I can tell you is what the evidence shows. I have no window into the mind of a burglar. Perhaps they didn't know much about art — chose a shop to rob at random and then got scared off before they could take anything more.' Wilberforce shrugged. 'There's no indication that the victim tried to call for help before he died — his phone's still in his pocket, and the landline handset's out of reach and on the cradle — so it must have been quick. And I can't tell you much more than that until we have some results from the lab. But . . .'

'But you don't like the look of it?'

'No, Sergeant, I don't. And I don't like the smell of it, either.'

* * *

Dr Raymond Dunwoody, now divested of his medical suit, sat in the middle gallery with DS Edwards and PC Crane. They had arranged themselves on a banquette facing a wall of shriekingly colourful abstract paintings. Did Louis Gillette own all this art, or was he just an intermediary — displaying art and selling it for the artists? And if it was his, who would inherit all this stuff, and what they would do with it?

'On the face of it, it looks like a heart attack,' said Dunwoody. 'He could have knocked over that bronze statue of Apollo that Jen Wilberforce showed you in his death throes. Or it could be as Jen says — someone grabbed it to threaten or fight off someone else.' He noticed Crane was scribbling in his notebook and added, 'Mind, it was Jen Wilberforce who said the statue was Apollo. I wouldn't have had the faintest what it was.'

Glyn Edwards thought of the gallery's owner, still lying dead in the neighbouring room, and had the sudden uneasy fantasy that in a moment he would come to join them on the banquette.

'There was a strong smell in that room,' said DS Edwards. 'Peaches and alcohol.'

'Yes, there was.'

'And no obvious source for the smell.'

'Some of it was coming from the body, and possibly some from a sink in the washroom at the back of the gallery. SOCO have taken some samples, but I'm not sure they'll find much. I can't confirm till I've done the post-mortem, but it smelled very much as if Louis Gillette had drunk some kind of peach liqueur before his death. Did you recognise the decedent, Glyn?'

'No. Obviously, I knew who he was, but I've never been to this gallery before. I'm not much interested in art.'

'Well, although you don't much care for Art, you've now seen *Still life, with Statue of Apollo*. Oh dear, not in the best of taste, perhaps! There's something very odd about Louis Gillette's death. You saw the cherry red flush on his skin?'

'I did. And if we put that together with the strong smell of liquor, but no bottle or glass, that suggests—'

'Let's not get ahead of ourselves, Glyn. We can't be certain how he died until I've opened him up and run some tests. The ambulance should be here within minutes to take him down to the morgue.'

'How long has he been dead?'

'Well, rigor mortis is still quite pronounced. I'd say he's been dead for what? Five hours. Five and a half.'

'So, he died about five o'clock this afternoon, while the Arcade was still open. PC Crane, go and look at the opening hours pasted on the door. I saw them as we came in. Find out when the gallery was supposed to close. Who informed the police?'

'The night security guard. Apparently, a friend of Gillette's, a man called Jack Prosser, came to see if he was all right, as his wife was worried about him.'

'Yes, PC Crane and I have just interviewed him.'

PC Crane returned from her errand. She looked excited.

'Sergeant,' she said, 'the gallery's open from nine a.m. to six p.m., closed Wednesdays and Sundays. Which means—' She paused in embarrassment. She was a uniform. It wasn't her job to go making suggestions.

'Yes, go on, Constable. What does it mean?'

'Sir, if Mr Gillette was dead by five p.m., as Dr Dunwoody says, then he wouldn't have shown the *CLOSED* sign in the window, because there was an hour of business left. So you were right, sir. The burglar turned that sign round as they left the premises, so that no one would go in and find the body before they'd made themself scarce. Or maybe they turned it round when they entered the gallery, so that nobody would interrupt. A cool customer, sir.'

'And it also means that our burglar wasn't afraid of running into the owner of the shop when they entered it — otherwise why not wait till after closing time?'

'Here's the ambulance,' said Dr Dunwoody. 'It won't take us many minutes to get the decedent out of here. After that, the place is all yours.'

* * *

'They've done a thorough job here, PC Crane,' said Glyn Edwards. 'See all those little white spots everywhere? They've gone to town looking for fingerprints.'

PC Crane was examining the open safe.

'This safe really *is* empty, sir,' she said. 'No papers, ledgers, or anything like that. Maybe he just kept a cash box in there and was putting the day's takings in it when the burglar struck, and made away with it. The cash box, I mean.'

'Hm . . . I wonder how much was in that cash box. Well, there's nothing here for us, Constable. What did you say your name was?'

'PC Crane, sir.'

'No, I mean your Christian name.'

'Anita, sir.'

'Well, Anita, like I said, there's nothing here for us. The SOCOs have the gallery's computer. But we're not done yet. We need to speak to that security guard. Did you take down his name?'

PC Crane flicked open her notebook. 'Kevin Marshall,' she said.

'It's getting a bit late,' said Glyn, 'so let's go and find this Kevin Marshall, who'll be in his office. I rather think he can be prevailed upon to brew us all a cup of tea.'

* * *

'He was a lovely man, Mr Edwards,' said Kevin Marshall. 'Very kind, and nicely spoken, but with no side on him, if you know what I mean. I can't imagine what happened. Who'd want to kill a nice man like Mr Gillette?'

Marshall, a strongly built man with a shaven head, appeared far more like a policeman than Glyn had when he'd looked in the mirror that morning, but of course he wasn't: he was a civilian, lacking any powers of arrest and detention. The three of them sat in Marshall's little office, drinking strong tea from plastic cups. It was close on midnight.

'Have the scene-of-crime team asked you for the CCTV footage yet, Mr Marshall?' asked Glyn.

Marshall shook his head sadly. 'They did, but I'm afraid I had nothing to give them. The cameras have been broken all week — we're waiting on an engineer to come out and fix them.'

Glyn let out a small cry of annoyance. 'I don't suppose you were here earlier today, you being on night duty?'

'Oh, yes, I was here this afternoon — about three, it would have been — because I knew that the day man — Sam Jones — would appreciate a bit of help.'

He pointed to the banner stretching across the Arcade. 'Today was our big autumn sale day,' he said. 'All the shops have really good bargains, and the place is crowded all day.

You can't move in here by twelve. So I was glad to come in and give Sam a hand. Stoddard's did very well. They always have massive reductions on engagement and wedding rings in the autumn sale.'

'I don't suppose the Rembrandt Gallery had a sale?'

'Well, no, Mr Gillette never joined in the sale days. He wasn't stuck up or anything, but he considered himself a cut above the average shopkeeper. God! It doesn't bear thinking of.'

Glyn Edwards thought, *So the place was thronging with people all day, and our thief could just have mingled with the crowd, slipped into the gallery, and turned the OPEN notice round to CLOSED. A bit of a gamble? Perhaps.* But it had evidently paid off. The thief had gone there bent on murder, he felt sure of that — why else enter the room when Louis Gillette was certain to be there?

'What happened to the man who discovered the body?'

'Jack Prosser? I know who he is, on account of him being games teacher at the high school, where my younger sister Ashley goes. He came here about half past nine, and I let him in. I knew who he was, but I didn't let on. Schoolteachers get embarrassed if you say you know them.

'Anyway, it would have been close on ten when he came running across the empty Arcade and into this office. He looked ghastly, and he was trembling. He told me that he'd discovered Mr Gillette lying dead, and that he'd been murdered. I sat him down in that chair and rang the police at Central.'

'So he definitely said murdered, hm? Well, it's getting late, time for us all to go. You've been very helpful, Mr Marshall. Thanks for the tea. Poor Mr Gillette's safe in the mortuary now, so we'll see what the medical examiner can tell us tomorrow.'

3. THE SECRET CACHE

'I can't believe he's dead,' said Lydia Gillette to her friend
Chloe McArthur. Her voice came small and low as she
uttered the words. Of course he was dead! Jack had come to
her well after midnight and had told her the appalling news
— that he had found the body and he thought it looked like
murder. He had been quite unable to comfort her, as he was
in such a sorry state that it had been all he could do to give
her a coherent account of what he had seen.

He had left her after half an hour, white and trembling.
He had given her a swift kiss on the cheek, but had made no
attempt to hold her close, or even say that he was sorry for
what had happened.

The police were not long in following — some sergeant
or other who apologised with his words but not his tone of
voice for the lateness of the hour, and a young constable,
unpleasantly alert. All she'd wanted to do was get them out
of the house — she could barely remember a thing they'd
said, except that they had seemed less sure about the cause of
death than Jack had been.

She had phoned her father in London and stammered
out the dreadful news. He made no attempt to solicit further
information from her but said that he would catch an early

train from Euston and be with her as soon as possible in the morning. She had made herself a cup of cocoa and curled up under a coat on one of the oatmeal sofas. Before she had fallen into a fitful sleep, she had forced herself to ask the awful question: what had Jack done? There could have been no love lost between him and her husband, so why had he shown such — such wild grief? Or was it *fear*?

Getting up from the sofa at eight o'clock, she had made herself presentable, and at nine o'clock there came a ring at the door. She opened it to admit her three closest friends from the Cathedral Ladies' Guild. They had come uninvited, but she was pleased and relieved to see them.

They had all done what they could to be with her in her numbed and guilty grief. They were real friends in need, whom she had known for years, Claudia Hurst, bossy but sensible, who had once been the cathedral librarian, and now worked as a librarian and archivist in Bishop Poindexter's collections; Felicity Campbell — dear, strong Felicity! — whose own husband, the archdeacon, had died not long ago; and Chloe McArthur, not just a loyal friend, but a licensed detective . . .

She didn't much care for Chloe's professional partner, Noel Greenspan. He was a kindly man, but rather overbearing, and given to spouting reams of poetry. She had no time for show-offs.

Claudia Hurst and Felicity Campbell went into the kitchen, and very soon returned with quantities of tea and toast. Talking to these three friends did much to calm her down, though she felt sick with horror. What harm had Louis ever done her, apart from failing in his duties as a husband? What would her friends think of her if they knew that she was an adulteress?

Adulteress, fornicator. Old-fashioned words for eternal truths that modern fashion and secularism could not erase. The guilt kept intruding. She'd gone through a phase of quoting the Bible when her affair with Jack had started, until the others had started giving her concerned looks. Now, if she wasn't careful, she'd turn into Noel Greenspan and start spouting poetry.

'My father will be here soon,' she said. 'I phoned him last night.'

'That's splendid, Lydia,' said Claudia Hurst. 'I'm going now to do a whole pile of shopping for you. If you feel that you'd welcome some help about the house, I know a number of people who could come out to you on a daily basis.'

Felicity Campbell, an impressive woman who, in her widowhood, had begun to run a refuge for battered women, took Lydia's hand, and looked at her gravely.

'You'll be angry and shocked out of yourself for a long time, Lydia,' she said, 'but you will survive. I don't think I'll ever get over losing my husband, but I'm coming to terms with my loss, and I hope you'll call me if you need some support. You know where to find me if you want me. Just ring, any time of night or day, and I'll come to you.'

When the two women had gone, Chloe and Lydia went into the kitchen to wash up the tea things. It was looking a little dated, Lydia thought sadly — she had had it done up in the nineties, not long after she'd married, and hadn't got around to updating it since.

'Chloe,' said Lydia Gillette, 'what will happen now? The police came to talk to me last night — a thin sad-looking detective and a nosey constable in uniform — but I was distraught and didn't really listen to them properly. But I'd like to know when they'll be back. Surely, they'll want to see me, and show me Louis's body to identify? They'll ring, won't they?'

'They'll ring and then they'll come here to Gladstone Road, I expect. The investigating officer — from your description it sounds like Detective Sergeant Edwards — will come here with his boss, Detective Inspector French. They'll ask you some questions, and then take you into town to view the body.'

'Will he . . .' She drew in a breath and started again. 'Will they have cut him open?'

30

'No, they will ask you to identify the body before the post-mortem.' Chloe saw the look on her friend's face and added, 'It will just look as though Louis is sleeping.'

What would they think of her, if they knew? Knew about her and Jack Prosser?

It had been years now since Louis had shared any information about the business with her. There were days when he would be gloomy and silent in the evenings, others when he seemed full of cheerful optimism. But he told her nothing. He would go into his private room upstairs and sit at his desk, muttering and fuming to himself. What secrets had he kept from her? And how dare she talk of secrets, when she herself had been living a furtive double life? Chloe was a private investigator; she could help.

* * *

'Chloe, I want you to look through Louis's papers and letters in his little bureau upstairs. I know the police will probably take everything away, but I want you to look at them first, in your professional capacity. I couldn't bear to do it. You might see something there that could give you a clue to why my husband is dead. I know you're good with documents of all sorts. Will you do that for me, now?'

Chloe McArthur looked at the grieving widow. Svelte and elegant, Louis had described her as 'fragile' when they had met at the exhibition the previous Tuesday. It was true that Lydia had never worked or supported herself — Chloe had often wondered if she had a hidden illness that prevented her from getting about, but Louis had seemed to be talking about mental fragility. Still, she had known Lydia for years and had often thought she had hidden wells of strength.

'You understand, don't you, Lydia, that I can't remove anything from that desk? Everything must be left for the police to find. But yes, I'll look through Louis's things for you. The police will already have taken all documents and

31

files from Louis's office in the gallery. Show me this desk, and I'll get to work.'

Lydia took her up to a room on the first floor, a room with barred windows, looking out on to a forlorn garden where everything seemed to be neglected and abandoned.

'This was a nursery, originally,' said Lydia. 'Hence the ancient bars on the windows — I've always wanted to update it, but Louis liked the old-fashioned style. There's the rolltop desk where Louis kept his papers. It isn't locked. He never kept it locked. I'll leave you for a while, if that's all right.'

There were six small drawers and a central pigeonhole. One drawer contained a packet of letters, once secured by a now perished elastic band. A quick glance told Chloe that these were in Lydia's handwriting; love letters? She would tell Lydia that they were there.

The other drawers held various business letters and invoices, all to do with the house rather than the gallery, some of them years old. There were receipted tradesmen's bills, various estimates for decoration and repairs, and advertisements for double glazing, with sums worked out on them in pencil. Nothing dramatic or exciting. Chloe arranged all these documents by order of date, and saw that the last invoice, for replacing two rotten windowsills, was from August 2014. Perhaps more recent debts had been paid in cash or in kind, or he'd switched to paperless invoices. She looked around but couldn't see a computer. Small businesses were pretty mobile nowadays — he probably used the same laptop for work and home and had it with him when he was killed. She wondered if the police or the burglar had it now.

There was a cash box in the centre pigeonhole, its key still in the lock. It contained sixty pounds in ten-pound notes, a Scottish twenty-pound note, and six one-pound coins.

There was nothing in the desk that could be of any interest to the police, but no doubt they would take everything away to examine. But the desk, she saw, was at least a hundred years old, made at a time when there was a minor craze for 'secret' drawers. (Hardly secret, she thought, as the buyer had to be told how to locate them, and everybody in the workshop would have known how to do that.) Chloe felt around the sides of the pigeonhole until she found what felt like a knot in the wood. When she pressed it, the bottom of the alcove slid to one side, revealing a sizeable cavity. Yes!

Inside, she found a letter from Oldshire Estates, dated 8 August, demanding that three months' arrears of rent for the Rembrandt Gallery be paid immediately, or the matter would be placed in the hands of the Estate's solicitors. Chloe recalled the young man who had accosted Louis Gillette at the gallery, threatening legal action; had he been an emissary of Oldshire Estates? Why was this letter in the secret drawer? So that Lydia would not see it. Chloe felt convinced that her friend had no idea of her husband's financial plight.

There was a letter, still in its envelope, from a Mr J. Hollingworth, of St Paul's Flags, London W1, assessor for the art and antique trades.

> *Dear Mr Gillette,*
>
> *I have now examined the painting that you sent to me, which you described as an Italian primitive, either by Giotto or from his workshop. It is a beautifully executed work, but I have to tell you that it is a copy, created by John Partridge in the nineteenth century. This man always left his initials, J.P., on an inner edge of the canvas behind the frame, which he has done in this case. I recently had to tell Lord Renfield, who lives in your part of the world, that his Van Dyke was also one of John Partridge's copies. I am so sorry to disappoint you. My bill for £400 will follow soon.*
>
> *I do hope that you did not pay a great deal to acquire this work. There is an esoteric market for such things, and I could get you £200 for it if you care to leave it with me.*

Scrawled across the letter in red ballpoint Gillette had written: *I paid £90,000 for it!*

There was a sheet of note paper, folded in half, and scuffed around the edges, as though it had been stuffed into a pocket for some time before ending up in the secret cache. It contained a simple message, with no greeting or signature.

Why not try M? If you want, I'll put in a word for you.

There were three advertisements cut from newspapers and held together with a paper clip, all for beauty salons, two in Newcastle and one in Gateshead. They had been inserted loosely into a pocket guide to Newcastle.

Finally, Chloe found a single sheet of Louis's own headed writing paper — for the house in Gladstone Road, not the gallery. Written on it several times, as though the writer were trying out a new pen, was the name Donald Wainwright.

The doorbell rang, and presently Chloe heard Claudia Hurst talking to Lydia. Evidently, she had just returned with the shopping. Chloe snapped a few pictures with her mobile phone of all the documents that she felt might be of interest. She put everything back where she had found it and closed the desk.

When she got downstairs, she found that Claudia Hurst had left. She joined Lydia in the kitchen, where she was unpacking the groceries. Lydia looked even more ravaged with grief than she had been earlier that morning.

'Well?' she asked tremulously.

'Lydia, Louis might have been in debt. He owed three months' rent on the gallery, among other things. He had also bought what he thought was a very valuable painting for ninety thousand pounds—'

'What? Where on earth could he have found a sum like that? Where is this painting?'

'I don't know, but there was a letter from an art expert in London, telling Louis that the painting was a copy, with a curiosity value of two hundred pounds.' Chloe hesitated for a moment, and then said, 'Lydia, is this house mortgaged?'

'No, it is ours outright. Oh! Do you think Louis may have re-mortgaged it, to try to pay off this debt? I don't think he could do that without telling me, could he? I can't understand it. He's been quite buoyed up this last week or so, and I thought the gallery must have been doing well.'

'Get on to your solicitor and your bank as soon as you can, Lydia. You'll need to see Louis's will and find out about that mortgage. But first, you must prepare yourself to identify poor Louis's body, and talk to the police.'

There was one thing for which Lydia could be thankful, thought Chloe, despite her lack of independent spirit. Her father, Simon Bolt, was a very rich man, and his daughter would never lack for support. If Louis had re-mortgaged the house, Lydia's father would redeem it immediately.

A taxi drew up at the house and, in a moment, there was a furious ringing of the bell. Lydia ran to the door, opened it, and a whirlwind of a man erupted into the hall. He was well over seventy, so far as Chloe could judge, but seemed to have the vitality of someone much younger. He was dressed very formally in a dark suit with matching tailored overcoat, and wore a dark Homburg hat. He had a large head, a florid complexion, and bright, belligerent blue eyes.

Simon Bolt folded his daughter in a bear-like embrace and kept her close while he looked at Chloe McArthur with an expression that clearly said, 'Who are you, and what are you doing here?'.

'My name's Chloe McArthur, Mr Bolt. I'm one of Lydia's friends.'

'Pleased to meet you. So my son-in-law has been murdered!'

His booming voice seemed to shake the brilliants in the chandelier. Lydia pulled away from him.

'Oh, well, the police aren't sure yet,' she said, wringing her hands.

'I'd be surprised if it was murder. When you called I thought you were going to say he had committed suicide—'

'Oh, Daddy, how could you say such a thing? I haven't even seen — seen his body, yet, and you're saying horrid things about him. You never liked him.'

'Well, my girl, I'd every reason not to like him. I wasn't going to mention this yet, but Buckley — you know my financial advisor? — gave me incontrovertible proof last week that your precious Louis had defrauded me of a million pounds. I was taking steps to deal with him, but it's too late, now. But that money must be somewhere, and I aim to find out where. Oh, there, don't take on so. What's done is done. But in God's name, what was Louis up to?'

Simon Bolt looked round the room as though appraising it for a sale catalogue. Maybe he was, thought Chloe.

'Are you going to stay here, Lydia,' he boomed, 'or would you like to move into a hotel? Well, please yourself. I'll be staying at the Church Eaton Hotel, but I'll be with you for all this unpleasantness at the mortuary, and any interview with the police. I'll not let my daughter be bullied by anybody! I must pay a quick visit to the bathroom.'

Lydia's father plunged up the stairs. Lydia, ashen-faced, took Chloe by the arm.

'He swindled Daddy out of a million pounds! And found ninety thousand from somewhere to pay for a dud picture! Oh, Chloe, you're a detective. Would you and Noel look into it for me? Professionally, I mean. Trace the creditors for me and find out whether they're willing to accommodate. I can't just sit back and let Daddy bear the burden of all those secret debts.'

'Are you quite sure that's what you want, Lydia? You understand, don't you, that Noel and I will not stop until we've brought the whole truth to light? We won't try to hide anything or suppress anything.'

'Do all that you have to, Chloe. Then I can concentrate on burying my husband.'

'A couple of questions, then. Does the name Donald Wainwright mean anything to you?'

'No, I don't think so. Who is he?'

'I'm not sure. It's a name I found scribbled on some paper upstairs.' Chloe thought for a moment. 'Did Louis have any kind of connection with Newcastle? Or Gateshead?'

'Not to my knowledge. *Newcastle*?' Lydia was at a loss.

The sound of the toilet flushing sent Chloe for the door — she didn't intend to spend half the day explaining herself and her fees with Simon Bolt's hostile gaze trained upon her. 'Well, we'll leave it there, Lydia. I'll email you our fee structure, and if you're happy with that then I'll get the investigation underway. Meanwhile, you know where your friends are to be found, and you've got your father to be with you at this terrible time.'

'I'll die of shame, Chloe, when people hear that Louis was a swindler.'

They heard another car stop in the road outside. Chloe looked out of the window and saw DI French and DS Edwards walking towards the house. At the same time, Simon Bolt came bounding down the stairs to join them in the hall.

* * *

Greenspan and McArthur, Private Detectives, occupied first-floor premises in Canal Street, a decidedly downmarket area of Oldminster, in a tangle of Victorian streets stretching between the canal and the railway station. The office was a sterile, neon-lit suite of two rooms and a cloakroom, the walls painted a uniform magnolia. All the floors were covered in beige carpet, but what the place lacked in imagination it made up for in its general air of cleanliness and efficient tidiness.

The only untidy item in the room was Noel Greenspan himself. An unkind friend had told him that he was 'running to fat', and it was true that he had started to develop a double chin. His business suits always looked crumpled, and Chloe was constantly nagging him to take them to Salters the Cleaners in the High Street.

It was the Monday after the death of Louis Gillette.

'She'd no idea', said Chloe McArthur, 'that her husband was not only hopelessly in debt, but an embezzler. He'd swindled her father out of a million pounds. I felt that she was more affected by the shame of that embezzlement than she was by her husband's death. Then again,' she went on, 'Lydia has what I'd call a very decided moral standpoint — she's rather old-fashioned in some ways. She got quite tight-lipped when she found out about the Roberts's break-up.'

'When Jane Roberts left her husband for the tennis coach, you mean?'

'Yes. She came out with an obvious excuse to avoid Jane when she returned for a visit last year, and they'd been quite close before that. Jane told me Lydia hadn't returned any of her messages since the news was made public.'

'Perhaps she was just upset Jane hadn't told her sooner.'

'Maybe.' Chloe looked thoughtful. 'But she did start talking about the ten commandments after that — lots of "thou shalt not's". I know we met through church, but it's not like we were on a Bible discussion group, is it? I thought it a bit much.'

Noel watched with affection as Chloe unpacked a batch of papers from her bag and shuffled them into order. They were partners in life as well as business partners, and Noel had often asked her to marry him, in his clumsy way, but Chloe seemed to like the arrangement as it stood — a shared business and separate houses, facing each other across a Regency-era garden square. But then, Noel's first marriage had ended in divorce; perhaps Chloe thought it safer to keep things as they were.

He suppressed a sigh. They were quite different people, in many ways, he reminded himself, and what worked in the office might well not work at home. He sat behind a desk with his back to the window, a desk piled up with yearbooks and directories, cardboard files, a little carriage clock, and an array of knick-knacks, including a row of lead soldiers and an ashtray made of plasticine. Chloe favoured a plain table, Formica-topped, and holding an Apple iMac. She kept her data here, whereas Noel's preference was to have two filing cabinets, standing to the right of his desk.

'You knew Louis Gillette, too, didn't you?' said Noel. 'In fact, you went to that exhibition of his the other day. How did he seem to you?'

'He seemed very happy, very optimistic. He quoted some poet or other about God being in his heaven. He didn't seem to me like a man who was going to be murdered.'

Noel screwed up his eyes and quoted from memory.

The year's at the spring
And day's at the morn;
Morning's at seven;
The hillside's dew-pearled;
The lark's on the wing;
The snail's on the thorn:
God's in his heaven—
All's right with the world!

'That's how Louis Gillette felt, was it? That's a famous verse from a play by Robert Browning. Not quite like a man who's going to be murdered, or . . .'

'Or commit suicide? I didn't know him well, Noel, but he did not strike me as being the suicidal type. No, I'd be tempted to think that he died from natural causes brought on by the shock of the burglar, if it wasn't for the oddness of the timing — they say the burglar arrived before closing time. And I heard something very odd when he was talking to someone on the phone at the gallery that night. He said, "No choice but murder? You actually heard him say that?" But then he went on to say that whoever said those words had just written him a very nice letter. So it's probably not important, but it made me wonder.'

'Is there still uncertainty over the cause of death?' asked Noel. 'Haven't they done the post-mortem yet?'

'It is awkward dying over the weekend, isn't it? Hardly anyone on call to process your body. But I got the feeling they were prioritising this case. DI French was looking very grave when he arrived at Lydia's house on Saturday — that's always a sign he thinks something is up. When I saw the look on his face, I insisted on going to the mortuary with Lydia,' Chloe continued. 'Louis was in a little room with a spotlight trained on him. He was lying on a sort of bed and looked as though he was gently sleeping. I'm afraid she took the viewing very badly, even so.'

'And Paul French wanted the post-mortem prioritised?'

'That's the feeling I got. Paul French is keeping this very close to his chest. He just said that he'd release the full results of the post-mortem tomorrow or Wednesday. He gave me that special look of his that means, "Don't push it". There's something very peculiar going on. Poor Lydia had to spend Sunday sitting at home knowing nothing. Claudia Hurst was with her for most of the day.'

'And Lydia Gillette's father is Simon Bolt, the entrepreneur? Let's find out about him.'

Noel picked up one of the directories and began to sift through the pages.

'Yes, here he is. Native of London. Born 1943, so he's what? Seventy-five. Grammar school . . . technical college. Entrepreneur and trader in mineral futures. Hm . . . Thought to be worth a great deal. Children: Lydia Gillette. Sole heir, eh? Did he marry her for the money?'

'I didn't know them back then, but I had always thought it was a love match. I've never thought badly of Louis before — he spoke of Lydia affectionately to me the last time I saw him. But I was there when Mr Bolt told us that Louis had swindled him out of a million pounds. He said that he'd go after the money. Perhaps we can get there first!'

Chloe unlocked a drawer in her desk and removed a folder containing print-outs of the photos of the various documents that she had discovered in Louis Gillette's secret drawer. She'd learnt long ago that it wasn't worth trying to show Noel anything on a screen; he would just complain about the resolution or the glare.

'There was nothing of any interest in the desk itself,' she said, 'but these documents must have had some very secret meaning for Louis Gillette for him to have hidden them there in the secret drawer.'

'Hm . . . Well, let's see what we've got here. I shall need my magnifying glass, as these prints are not very clear.'

Chloe sighed. Evidently Noel was playing out his fussy old man character. Still, that was preferable to his Sherlock Holmes impersonation.

'Ah! This letter from Oldshire Estates — he owed three months' rent on the gallery, and they were starting to insist on payment. Why hide it, though? Probably so that Lydia wouldn't see it. Evidently she didn't know about the secret compartment in the desk.'

'When I was at the exhibition that Tuesday, I saw a young man talking urgently to Louis, in effect telling him that legal action for restitution would be commenced if he didn't pay his debt. I can't be entirely certain, but I'm sure he'd come from Oldshire Estates.'

'Pressing debts can lead to two unpleasant conclusions,' said Noel, 'either absconding or suicide. Not, as in this case, murder. Very interesting.'

'Or further debt,' pointed out Chloe. 'That's three. Or paying off the debt by winning on the horses or the lottery. Would that be classed as pleasant or unpleasant?'

'What?'

'You said two unpleasant conclusions.'

Noel picked up another print, a little discomfited by Chloe's light-hearted tone, and peered at it through his hand lens.

'That's the letter from Hollingworth, the art expert,' Chloe explained.

'So Gillette was a victim of a prolific Victorian art copier. And he'd paid ninety thousand pounds for the painting! Where did he get a sum like that — is it the money he "swindled" from his father-in-law? And more to the point, who sold him the fake Giotto? Perhaps we could put out a few feelers there.

'You know, Chloe, for an art dealer, Louis Gillette seems to have been a bit of an amateur. Wouldn't he get the painting examined by a specialist before handing over ninety thousand? What else is there? Ah! This is very interesting! A message written on a piece of paper: *Why not try M? If you want, I'll put in a word for you.* Your observations, please, Chloe.'

'If it was kept in the secret drawer, it was because Louis Gillette didn't want his wife to see it. That suggests to me that "M" must be yet another moneylender. Noel, all these things seem to be stages on the road to suicide, and yet I feel sure from Paul French's attitude on Saturday that it was murder.'

They sat in silence for a minute, listening to the humming of a mini-fridge in one corner of the room. It was Noel Greenspan who broke the silence.

'I find myself coming up with all sorts of possibilities,' he said.

'What do you mean?'

'In the absence of facts, we could say it was suicide or murder, or natural causes, or suicide dressed up as murder.'

'Don't you mean murder dressed up as suicide? That's the norm in detective novels, isn't it?'

They smiled at each other.

'Perhaps we should just focus on the evidence before us.' Noel picked up his hand lens again. 'Now, let's see what's left. Two adverts for beauty salons in Newcastle, and one in Gateshead. Nothing secret about those: there's their addresses and telephone numbers — all landlines, I note. Established businesses. And yet they were in the secret drawer . . . And now a photograph of a guide to Newcastle . . . And finally, here's a piece of paper with a name written on it several times: Donald Wainwright. Come on, Ms McArthur, put it all together, and tell me what it means.'

'It looks like a man practising a new signature, trying to give individuality to a name that's not his own. And the advertisements, harmless enough in themselves, but dangerous if seen by prying eyes . . . A new identity? Possibly venturing into a new line of business? I don't know . . .'

'A man, up to his eyes in debt, who was about to make a bolt for it. Was Louis Gillette about to start a new life in the north? Well, it's a working hypothesis.'

'Lydia couldn't possibly have known anything about it.'

'You say that, Chloe, because she's your friend. She may know everything about it, and was planning to join Gillette in his new life when the time was ripe. Or, as you say, she may be entirely innocent. Well, the game's afoot, and the best way to start this investigation is to go after the money.'

* * *

Deep in the interior of a 1930s complex of shops and first-floor flats facing one side of an area known as the Triangle, was to be found the surgery of Mr Brooke Cliveden, Oldminster's premier chiropodist. At the end of a carpeted passage in a kind of Aladdin's cave of a place, a comfortable waiting area led to Mr Cliveden's workplace. The walls of the waiting area were plastered with children's paintings and drawings, and there were copies of magazines to read while you waited your turn. The place was never crowded, as all visits were by appointment. Prominent among the children's artwork was a printed sign which proclaimed: 'Hell hath no fury like a woman's corns'.

Sister Maureen Kennedy came into the Aladdin's cave on Monday afternoon and found that Mr Cliveden was ready and waiting to treat her, much to her annoyance. She had arrived early, looking forward to her usual fifteen-minute chat with Gertrude, the receptionist, and a cup of tea — she didn't much like having her feet touched, but it was a necessary evil that Gertrude's harmless chatter made more bearable.

Mr Brooke Cliveden always looked the same: a distinguished, silver-haired man in his seventies, quietly spoken and uncannily skilled. He had kept her corns and callouses under firm control for more years than Sister Maureen cared to remember. There he sat, surrounded by the instruments of his profession, nippers and cutters, scalpels and blades, files and probes, burrs and discs . . . Sister Maureen suppressed a shudder.

'So what do you think of poor Mr Gillette's murder?' asked Brooke Cliveden, as he inspected Sister Maureen's feet.

'A dreadful, wicked thing, Brooke. I shall pray for the repose of his soul, God rest him. His poor wife will be heartbroken, but I know she's got some good friends at the cathedral who'll do their best to help her.'

Brooke Cliveden switched on a whirring brush and got to work. Sister Maureen gritted her teeth and tried not to twitch her feet.

'I don't suppose she'll be coming to your embroidery classes for a while, now,' he said.

'Embroidery classes? No, Mrs Gillette's never been to them.'

'I thought she went to them on Tuesday evenings. That's what she—'

Mr Cliveden stopped speaking abruptly and gave all his attention to his patient's foot. Sister Maureen thought: *Well, now, Lydia Gillette's being telling Mr Cliveden fibs. He won't betray her — of course he won't — and I'll not pursue the matter.*

Towards the end of the afternoon Chloe McArthur arrived to have her feet tended to. This time, it was the patient, not the practitioner, who opened the proceedings.

'Oh, Brooke, have you heard what happened to Louis Gillette at the Rembrandt Gallery?'

'Yes, Chloe, I've been talking to Sister Maureen about it. A little bit of a mystery there. Lydia Gillette's another of my patients, and she told me that she attended embroidery classes at the Catholic church, but Sister Maureen says that isn't so. Maybe I've got the day wrong . . . But no, Sister Maureen said that she's never been to those classes. I don't know what to make of that. I said nothing to Sister Maureen, but as you're a particular friend of Lydia's, and a detective into the bargain, I thought I'd let you know.'

'I'm working for Lydia in a professional capacity,' said Chloe. 'I'm sure there'll be some simple explanation. Perhaps she goes to embroidery classes out of town.' *How lame that sounds!* she thought.

Matters turned professional, and they were both silent for a while. Then Brooke Cliveden spoke.

'Has Lydia told you much about her past? She came to Oldminster from London when she was ten,' he said, 'after her parents divorced. She and her mother came to live here because she had a cousin who taught French at the Ridley School for Girls. The father stayed in London to look after his various business concerns, or so they said. Lydia was very outgoing as a little girl and then as a teenager, but as she grew older, she became shyer and more reserved. She had some nice boyfriends, and everybody thought that in the end she'd settle down with a lad called Jack Prosser, who'd known her on and off ever since she came here. But no, she married Louis Gillette instead. People are funny, aren't they?'

'Jack Prosser . . . Isn't he one of the games teachers at Oldminster High? Maybe they'll come together again.'

'I doubt it,' said Brooke Cliveden. 'That father of hers — have you met him? Oh, you have? Well, you can see what a domineering kind of man he is. He'll come up with some way to put her off Jack, I've no doubt. That kind of man uses money like a weapon.'

'What happened to Lydia's mother?'

'She died when Lydia had just turned twenty. It was very sad — a case of septicaemia. Cut herself on a pair of garden shears, or so I heard. Lydia was never quite the same after that.'

Half an hour later, Chloe left the magical cave much refreshed and repaired, and faced the mundane realities of the Triangle and its many busy shops.

4. THE BRANDY TRAIL

'Louis Gillette was poisoned.'

Detective Inspector Paul French was a man in his late forties, quietly dressed in a dark suit of clerical grey, white shirt and Police Federation tie. He wore old-fashioned rimless glasses. Open on his desk was the final report on the autopsy conducted on the body of Louis Gillette. It was Tuesday, 18 September.

'Ray Dunwoody says here that Gillette was poisoned by the ingestion of prussic acid, which is another name for the liquid form of hydrogen cyanide. Apparently, the decedent's stomach was awash with it. That's the word Ray's used here. Awash.'

'I suspected something of the kind when I saw the body,' said Glyn. 'Gillette's face was flushed a kind of cherry red, one of the signs of cyanide poisoning. I could smell peaches and alcohol near his mouth, which suggests he was given the poison in something strong-smelling to mask the scent.'

'Murder, then.'

The two men were sitting in French's office in Jubilee House, the headquarters of the Oldshire Constabulary.

'It may have been suicide. Perhaps he just particularly liked the taste of a peach-flavoured liqueur and would rather taste that than the bitter almond taste of cyanide for his last drink. But then, who took the bottle he must have drunk from, and why?'

'Could he have drunk it somewhere else, or thrown the bottle out of the window?'

'I thought you said the room he was found in was windowless?'

'That's right, but couldn't he have—'

'I'm told it's unlikely he would have had time to move before the cyanide took effect, given how much he'd ingested. Ray Dunwoody says that apart from the prussic acid, the decedent's stomach was almost empty, which makes sense, as he'd probably had nothing much to eat since breakfast. He found a small quantity of masticated prawns. The people next door, the optician's, said that he often bought a sandwich from the lad who hawks them round the Arcade. Then Ray had the stomach contents subjected to a closer chemical analysis, and found the presence of yeast. What's yeast used for, Glyn?'

'To make bread rise when it's being baked. And it's in Marmite, isn't it?'

'Ray Dunwoody says that this particular yeast was *Saccharomyces* . . .?' French frowned at the page. 'Did I pronounce that right? I don't know how these chemists remember all these abstruse names. It's like gardening. Even a dandelion will have some fancy Latin name.'

'And this sacchawotsit — what's so special about it?'

'It's brewer's yeast, Sergeant Edwards. Something for us to ponder.'

'Did SOCO come up with anything interesting?'

'Just fingerprints and DNA, so far — Jack Prosser's and Louis Gillette's, of course, but also many others. They ran what they found through the databases but couldn't identify anyone else. But I did get a hit on the databases: our friend Jack Prosser's got form. Assault and battery when he was eighteen. Some row over a girl. Fined and bound over.'

'Well, well. We'd better have him in for further questioning. I felt at the time that his reaction to Louis Gillette's death was unusually severe. He was definitely hiding something or was afraid of something. He teaches PE at the high school. Shall we invite him round for a chat?'

'Central thought of that and went round to the school to see him this morning. But he wasn't there and had not turned up for work on Monday morning, either. Jack Prosser's in the wind.'

* * *

PC Anita Crane rather enjoyed foot patrol. It got her out of the stuffy interior of Central, a nondescript late Victorian building long in need of modernisation. It was hidden away from the more fashionable parts of Oldminster town centre, in a depressing cul-de-sac with the fanciful name of Lark Hill Rise.

Here she was, in the unnamed alley behind the fish market, a cobbled road to nowhere. It was the depository for all the trade bins, put out for collection on Thursday. And here, in the midst of them, slumped against a wall, was Sam Delaney, one of Oldminster's rough sleepers. He was half in and half out of a sleeping bag, a man with matted hair and beard, who could have been any age from thirty to sixty. His few possessions were arranged around him in plastic bags. He was fast asleep, a bottle of some liquor or other rolled against the wall beside him.

She'd have to move him on — the shopkeepers would begin calling in to report him soon if she didn't. Pity to wake him. He looked so calm and carefree, propped up against the wall, his ragged baseball cap drawn down over his eyes.

There was a smell of rotten fish from the market bins, and something else, something that stirred a memory. Peaches?

'Come on, Sam. Time to be moving.'

No reply. The smell of peaches and alcohol seemed very strong, just as it had been in Mr Gillette's gallery. PC Crane lifted Sam Delaney's cap, and found herself looking into a pair of dead, incurious eyes.

* * *

'Unreformed alcoholics like Sam Delaney will take a swig of anything from a bottle,' said Dr Raymond Dunwoody. 'Any bottle that looks as though it might contain alcohol.'

'PC Crane found the bottle in question beside him on the ground,' said DS Glyn Edwards. 'She also found the screw top, so when Sam found that bottle it was still stoppered. I agree with PC Crane that Sam had been rooting through the bins for anything salvageable and had found the bottle where the killer of Louis Gillette had abandoned it.'

Dr Dunwoody had called up DI French and DS Edwards to tell them the results of the post-mortem that he had conducted on the unfortunate rough sleeper just an hour after he had been found.

'Sam Delaney died from the ingestion of prussic acid,' said Dunwoody. 'There was a considerable quantity of the stuff in his stomach. I think he must have unscrewed the cap and chugged the whole contents down his throat in one go. He would have died within seconds.'

'Well,' said DI French, 'I think we can safely assume that Sam's death was an accident. But that lethal bottle lying beside him contains the poison used to murder Louis Gillette.'

'Our forensic people gave it a thorough going over,' said Glyn Edwards. 'It was a bottle of peach brandy — hence the smell of peaches, both in the gallery and in the alley behind the fish market.'

'I have been wondering about that. Was it used to mask the smell of cyanide, do you think?'

'Quite possibly. Cyanide has a distinctive bitter almond scent, and brandy on its own can hide it. Peach brandy would be even more effective, I expect. This particular brandy was a very high-class specimen, produced by the Californian vineyard of Lauretier Fils. It's known as "Grande Amber", and it's rarely found in the UK. You won't find it in Bargain Booze. Forensics found traces of the same kind of brewer's yeast as that present in poor Louis Gillette's stomach. Both men were killed by the contents of the same bottle.'

* * *

'I don't suppose it's of any consequence, Mr French,' said Eleanor Fox, 'but I thought you'd want to know. It was just before five o'clock on the day that Louis Gillette was murdered that I saw him. Of course, the Arcade was crowded, and I had quite a few people in my shop buying books, or thinking about buying them, and Gordon Caruthers, who helps me out on busy days, was quite capable of seeing to their wants, so I stepped out into the Arcade for a breath of air. It was very close, that day; at least I found it so.'

Eleanor Fox, proprietor of Fox's Bookshop at number 18, King's Arcade, was a neatly dressed, fastidious sort of woman in her forties, with sandy hair and a not very successful pince-nez. Paul French reckoned that the bookseller was feeling rather self-important at the thought of talking to an actual detective inspector in Jubilee House.

'What man was it that you saw?' asked French.

'Man?'

'You said "I saw him", so naturally—'

'Oh, yes, the man. Well, it was just before five o'clock, as I said, and I was standing outside my shop. I just happened to glance across towards the Rembrandt Gallery, and I saw this man open the door, and go in. He was a big, thickset kind of man, roughly dressed — though so many men these days dress badly, don't they? I think they do it on purpose, though why, I can't imagine. A man could dress himself with a bit of style and panache if he went to Currie's, at number sixteen. First-class tailoring for a very reasonable outlay. Mr Currie is my second cousin.'

'And this man . . . ?' said DI French heavily.

'Yes. He was thickset, as I said, not so young, but quick and decisive in his movements. He was carrying a large canvas holdall, blue, with tan leather handles, and I wondered rather idly whether he was going in to rob the gallery! A silly notion, really, but the man seemed out of place . . . He didn't look like the normal kind of shopper we get in here, people who pause to look in the windows, though young couples who come for Stoddard's sales tend to go straight up the Arcade to shop with them. Well, there it is. I expect it's nothing, but I thought you should know, because of the time, just before five, and poor Mr Gillette being murdered so soon after that.'

'I'm very grateful to you, Ms Fox,' said DI French. 'I think you may well have seen the murderer himself entering the shop. Did you form any theory about the holdall?'

Eleanor Fox looked pleased.

'How kind of you to ask! I really did think at first that he'd come to rob the gallery, and was about to phone Mr Gillette, but then I thought, how could you carry off a painting? It'd never get into a holdall. And if he just wanted the cash takings, there was no need for him to bring anything at all. But he did, you know, and he must have brought it for some purpose.'

French contained his sigh. Eleanor Fox would have called or even taken the time to pop into the gallery, surely, if she was worried about the man with the holdall or had wanted to show support for Louis. She must have built the whole thing up in her mind after the event — it happened with the best of eyewitnesses. This long after the day in question, he wasn't sure how useful her account would be. But he would have to get her to sign a statement, all the same.

'You're quite right, Ms Fox,' he said. 'And it will be up to us here at police headquarters to work out what that purpose was. I'm inclined to think that it might have been murder.'

* * *

Jack Prosser sat in a café at the gates of one of the bleak factories in Prior's Park Industrial Estate, planning his escape from Oldminster to the anonymity of London. At fifty-three his life was over. Last week a respected schoolteacher, he was now a fugitive, a man who needed to find himself a new identity, and some kind of under-the-counter work to keep body and soul together. He had plenty of money, but if he used an ATM to withdraw cash, the police would find him. And what about Lydia?

A cheerful girl brought him a bacon sandwich and a mug of tea.

Lydia . . . One day, somehow or other, he would find her again, but for the moment he must leave her to grieve alone. For she would grieve. Did she by now suspect that he had murdered Louis? Ever since that fatal Friday he had not been able to close his eyes without feeling the brandy glass in his hand, hearing the sickening crunch as he crushed it beneath his shoe.

The police would surely have figured it out by now. And he had a record. As a youth, he had got involved in a fight with another boy over a girl and had been fined and bound over. They would find it somewhere on a database and decide he was a bad character. He'd almost forgotten about the incident — it had been a lifetime ago.

He bit into the bacon sandwich, which proved to be very good. The tea was hot and strong. He had been a successful and popular teacher, and it would be a wrench never to see his colleagues and students again. He used to urge some of them to work harder, or they would end up stacking shelves in Robinson's supermarket. Now he would welcome the anonymity and security of a job stacking shelves.

In God's name, why had he done it? When he got home that night, he'd found peach brandy on his sleeve, still wet and cold, soaked into the fabric. He had showered, as though that would wash away his guilt. He had wrapped the jacket in a black plastic bag and put it in a wheelie bin outside the block of flats.

He thanked the waitress, leaving a pound coin on the table as a tip, and made his way out into what was proving to be a cold, wet evening. It was not quite dark, but the street-lights were on. Carrying his holdall, he walked past a factory yard where a man in a Day-Glo jacket was rolling a car tyre towards a vast collection of tyres piled up under a sort of open shed on one side of the yard. Lucky man! A job like that would do. Maybe he'd get lucky once he reached London.

The rain got heavier, but he'd not long to go. He didn't know this distant area of Oldminster at all. There seemed to be no houses, only factories, and miles of metal railings enclosing concrete yards. Kennedy Street. Longford Road. Churchill Way. Alien, unfamiliar places. He strove to conquer a rising despair as he trudged with his holdall through the rain.

At last!

Oldminster North train station. The eight thirty London train from Chichester stopped here, which was why he'd come out to this godforsaken part of town. Nobody would recognise him. He walked down the incline and into the empty booking hall, where he bought a single to London from the man behind the booking-office window. He automatically said, 'Good evening.'

The man replied darkly, 'It is for some!'

What did he mean by that?

The platform was deserted, and he stood there in the rain, waiting for the train to London Bridge. What seemed like hours was in fact only minutes, and soon he both saw and heard the train coming up the line. He could imagine stepping out of the rain and into the warmth of one of the lighted carriages.

A porter came out from the station building, holding a flag. He was accompanied by two men in jeans and bomber jackets, who walked slowly towards Jack Prosser where he stood in the rain. Act as though nothing was happening. Try to look nonchalant.

'You are Jack Prosser?' said one of the two men. 'We are police officers. You must come with us.'

53

'I'm glad it's over,' he said.

They didn't handcuff him, but they flanked him as they walked back up the slope and away to a waiting police car. As they reached it, Jack Prosser heard the London train starting up again for the journey that would have taken him to freedom.

* * *

Simon Bolt stepped out of the hired limousine and looked with quiet appreciation at Grace Hall. He liked these black-and-white timbered buildings, which had stood for hundreds of years, and Grace Hall was a gem of its kind. Bolt was a city man at heart, with a fine modern mansion in Chelsea together with an apartment at Tower Wharf, where his main offices were to be found. But he always relished a visit to his old business colleague Manfred Tauber at his subtly renovated Tudor mansion.

The forecourt was full of cars.

Ah! Here was the super-efficient Williams, Manfred's house manager.

'Welcome back to Grace Hall, sir,' he said. 'Mr Tauber's very busy today — the house is full of connoisseurs!'

'Nice to see you, Williams,' said Simon Bolt. 'I expect you know what's brought me down to this neck of the woods.'

'I do, sir. And I was very sorry to hear what happened. Let me take you through to Mr Tauber now. He's in the garden parlour.'

He followed Williams to an ancient chamber at the back of the house, a room with mullioned windows looking out on to a well-tended garden. The two rich men sized each other up as they shook hands. They were similar in build, large, domineering personalities, physically strong, and with a genius for business. Many years ago, they had been partners, but had long since gone their separate ways. Each was incalculably wealthy.

'So, Simon,' said Manfred Tauber, settling himself back in an ornate chair, 'you've lost your son-in-law to the hand of the assassin. Let me offer you my condolences.'

'You're too kind, Manfred, but he was no loss, I can tell you. I always thought Lydia was a fool marrying him, and now I find that he had swindled me out of a million pounds! I'd like to get it back. Oh, I'm sorry he's been murdered, of course; nobody deserves that. But he was a weak man, a failure, and a rogue.'

Simon Bolt's harsh voice echoed in the room. It was in marked contrast to the cultured tones of the man who liked to think of himself as the squire of Grace Hall. Manfred Tauber sat quite still in his chair, looking steadily at his former colleague.

'Did you lend him money, Simon, before you found out about this swindle, I mean? It never does to be indulgent in that way. That kind of debtor is a dangerous liability. Much wants more.'

'What would you have done?'

'I'd have let him go to the devil in his own way. But there you are. Perhaps he owed money to someone who was less indulgent than you are. Somebody who flew into a rage and murdered him. Things like that do happen.'

'No, he was poisoned — not exactly a heat-of-the-moment attack. Cyanide. It's a mystery to me how you could get a man to drink the stuff, but there it is. He did, and he's dead. Murdered.' He shook his head. 'Of course, my daughter is still spending money on the fool. She's hired a private investigator to look into his death and where the money went.'

'Has she! Is she spending the money, or are you? You need to watch these private investigators, my friend. They fleece you on expenses.'

'Oh, I'm not worried about that. The investigator in question is an old friend of hers and straight as a die — Chloe McArthur.' Bolt flashed him a smile. 'If it gives Lydia comfort, I don't mind subbing her the cash until she has her finances in shape.'

'Let me ring for Williams. You'll stay to lunch, won't you? I've got an excellent Hock, just in from Germany, which goes well with Scotch salmon.'

'Thank you. That would be very nice. You must think me very rude not to ask after Corinne. She's well, I trust?'

'She is. She's in London for a few days, doing a bit of shopping. To tell you the truth, I think she finds it rather dull out here in the sticks.'

'Williams told me that the house is full of connoisseurs. What did he mean by that? I saw a number of cars parked out at the front.'

'They've come to buy rare books from me, Simon. I have a vast collection here, and these folk come from time to time to make a purchase or two. Quite a coincidence that they should all choose to come on the same day! I'll ring for Williams.'

When the house manager arrived, Manfred Tauber told him to lay an extra place at table, as Mr Bolt was staying for lunch. When he had gone, Simon Bolt cleared his throat.

'I've sold out my holdings in the Baltic timber market,' he said, 'because it's not paying me enough. Those environment people are starting to be a nuisance, so I got out only this last week.' He looked at his hands and continued. 'Last time we spoke, Manfred, you said that you were putting together a consortium to organise a rapid trade in gilts at a time when nobody's interested in Government paper. I know what a wizard you are when you turn your mind to that sort of thing. What would you give me if I offered to join?'

'What are you prepared to invest?'

'The proceeds from selling out that Baltic timber interest: six million pounds.'

'I can give you seven per cent, compound, for five years, with no early redemption permitted. Full return of capital at redemption time.'

Simon Bolt nodded appreciatively, but Manfred Tauber had not quite finished.

'You do realise that this is a private consortium? Nothing should turn up in any accountant's report.'

'The money will come via my holding companies in Lichtenstein.'

'Excellent! Now let us go in to lunch. I'm sorry about that million your son-in-law stole from you. If I were you, I'd forget about it. Let it go, if only for your daughter's sake.'

'Well, maybe. But I don't like being swindled.'

* * *

Later that day, when both Simon Bolt and the visiting connoisseurs had departed, Williams sought out Danny O'Toole, the surly gardener.

'He's definitely back on form,' said Williams. 'He had them eating out of his hand today. All five of them arrived in the space of an hour, falling over themselves to buy some of his books. They'd all brought their cheque books. You remember that man Mario Goretti, who owns a string of Italian restaurants in London? His hand shook so much when he was writing his cheque that he had to sit down for a moment. Mr Tauber offered to get him a glass of brandy, which only made things worse. He managed to sign his cheque eventually, and went off with the book he'd bought, a second edition of one of Graham Greene's novels. The others just paid up, and left after lunch, clutching their various volumes.'

'Mr Bolt was there.'

'Yes, he and Mr Tauber go back a long way. Of course, he hadn't come to buy an old book!'

'Hm . . . Anyway, the boss took your advice about not going soft — you told him, didn't you, what I said? He's well and truly back on form. But watch him: all this country squire business could put him off his guard, and there are millions at stake.'

'More likely billions, Danny, if the truth be known.'

As he walked back to the house, he smiled to himself. Poor, quaking Mr Goretti's cheque for the Graham Greene novel had been for £26,000 . . .

* * *

'By saying nothing, Mr Prosser, you're only making matters worse for yourself. Your solicitor has told you that "No comment" could be seen as a refusal to tell the truth. Why were you trying to flee to London? What had you done to make you throw away a steady career as a respected school-teacher, and go on the run?'

'No comment.'

Jack Prosser sat next to his court-appointed solicitor, an elderly balding man in a pinstripe suit. DS Edwards faced them across the table in one of the bleak interview rooms in the basement of Jubilee House.

'We found your jacket in the bin outside your flat at Bankside. And what did we find on the sleeve? Peach brandy laced with cyanide — the very thing that killed Louis. You're an obstacle to the truth, and your actions are inexplicable. Why did you tamper with the crime scene? I don't think it was you who murdered him, was it?'

Jack Prosser hesitated for a moment, and then said, 'Murdered him?'

'Why not make a statement now? We want to eliminate you from the inquiry.'

The solicitor added his word. 'I would strongly advise you to do so, Mr Prosser.'

They both saw Prosser's indecision as he struggled to make up his mind. In the end, caution prevailed.

'No comment,' he said.

'Very well. This interview is over. You will now be remanded in custody on today's bench warrant and brought up before the magistrate at Crown Street Law Courts tomor-row, where we will ask for a further remand. Officer?'

Jack Prosser was led away to the cells, and the solicitor left to see another client. Glyn remained in the interview room, frustrated. What did it all mean? Was Jack Prosser shielding someone, an accomplice, perhaps, who scared him more than the police did? But apart from an adolescent brush with the law, he'd been an ideal citizen. A successful and popular teacher, so his colleagues said. Lived alone, but not a loner — good company. No one had a bad word to say about him.

There'll be something, thought Glyn. *You don't get into this kind of mess without there being a very good reason for it. Time will tell.*

* * *

'We're closed Saturday morning, Inspector, which is why I'm able to come and see you. I expect you know Mauleverer's Wine Merchants in Carlisle Street? We have a proud reputation of stocking only the finest wine and spirits, and our name is known to the most exacting oenophiles—'

'Oenophiles? What—'

'Wine lovers, you know. So, when a man came into my shop asking for a bottle of Lauretier Fils Grande Amber Peach Brandy, I gave him my full attention.'

Mr Mauleverer was a quietly dressed, gentlemanly sort of man, with a slow, deliberate mode of speaking. He wore gold-rimmed glasses, which magnified his pale blue eyes.

'It's very rare, you see,' he continued, 'so when this individual asked for a bottle — well, he didn't exactly ask, he thrust a scrap of paper at me with the name of the brandy written on it — I thought, will this poor looking man be able to afford it? I thought maybe he was an alcoholic. Anyway, he produced a fat envelope stuffed full of twenty-pound notes and paid for the brandy. He seemed a bit surprised when I wrapped up the brandy in tissue paper and placed it in a bag — quite a smart bag. He looked rather odd walking out of the shop with it. We've been reading all about the murder of Louis Gillette in the paper, and it mentioned this particular brandy by name, so I thought you should be told.'

'I'm very grateful to you, sir,' said DI French. 'Could you describe this man more clearly? You said he was "poor looking".'

'Yes, he was — well, I can actually tell you who he was, because my assistant said that she knew him, well, knew him by sight, at any rate. His name is Charles Deacon, and until recently he was living on benefits, but seems to have come into some money now. He may have been buying the brandy for himself, but to me he looked like the kind of man who'd prefer a crate of Guinness. So maybe he was buying it for someone else.'

When the wine merchant had gone, DI French thought, *Maybe he's right. We'd better have a word with this Charles Deacon.* Glyn Edwards would be back from the canteen in a few minutes. It was time to decide on a positive course of action.

5. TWO CONFESSIONS

Chloe McArthur tapped her fingers on her desk irritably. She had phoned Mr J. Hollingworth, art assessor, on Monday but he had been unable to help her discover the person who had sold Louis Gillette the fake Giotto. She had spent hours hunting for any hint of a moneylender known as 'M', but had turned up nothing. She could call her friend, the barrister Lance Middleton, QC, for some help — he had defended a few City ne'er-do-wells who might point him in the right direction — but he was much taken up with a court case at the moment, and she knew she shouldn't distract him until it had concluded.

So that left the clippings about the hairdressing businesses to look into. Those advertisements cut from newspapers, and that sheet of paper where Louis Gillette had practised writing the name 'Donald Wainwright' all suggested a man who was about to go on the run from his creditors and start a new life under an assumed name.

She sat in silence for a while, still drumming her fingers on the table, and then picked up the phone. She tried the one in Gateshead first.

'Hello? Is that Shelley's Unisex Salon? I believe you're up for sale, and I'd be interested — Oh, you're the new owner. Sorry to have bothered you. Goodbye.'

She hung up and dialled the next number.

'Hello, is that Barry's Stylists? I believe you're looking for a buyer, and I'd be very interested — Yes, I'm building up a folio of retail investments in Newcastle . . . I see, you're actually two businesses, the other being Brenda's Hair Heaven.'

She smiled. So there was no need to call the other number.

'I'd like to come up to Newcastle to see the premises if — Oh, there's already a prospective buyer, but he's not yet made a firm offer.'

Noel chose that moment to come into the room with the coffee.

She smiled her appreciation and continued to speak. 'I wonder whether that could be an associate of mine, Donald Wainwright? It is? Well, perhaps you'd like to wait until he makes an offer, or I can call on you to discuss a purchase. One of my people will be in Newcastle soon, and could call at your premises, if that's convenient.'

She set down the handset and took the cup of Blue Mountain coffee Noel handed to her.

'So,' said Noel, 'the game's afoot?'

Chloe suppressed a groan at the Sherlock Holmes impression. 'I wonder if Gillette meant to desert his wife, or was Lydia to join him later?'

'From what you've told me of Lydia Gillette and her "thou shalt not's", she wasn't likely to have taken him up on the offer.'

'Perhaps he was going to leave her. "She's fragile in so many ways and needs an understanding friend." That's what he said to me. I think he was saying she would need a good friend when he left her. I've begun to realise that Louis wasn't the good-hearted fool I thought he was, that's for sure.'

* * *

'If we don't charge Jack Prosser with a crime or misdemeanour, Glyn, we'll have to let him go,' said DI French. 'It's been four days, he's gone home and we've pulled him back in for questioning now. I can't make any sense of his refusal to talk.

We're not accusing him of murder, only of tampering with a crime scene.'

'And it was Prosser who alerted the security guard to the fact that murder had been committed,' said DS Edwards. 'So why did he go on the run? "I'm glad it's over," he said, when they arrested him at the station. That's what Christie the Rillington Place murderer said when *he* was arrested. Glad that *what* was over?'

'We're not going to find any answers just sitting here, Glyn. It's over a week now since Louis Gillette was murdered, and we know virtually nothing about who committed the crime. People are losing patience. Even the *Gazette*, which is normally pro-police, is starting to grumble. So we've got to look beyond that surly individual sitting in his cell in the basement.'

'What do you suggest, sir?'

'I was talking to Jack's wife Moira last night, and she told me that Lydia Gillette was telling lies about where she went every Tuesday evening. She got that bit of information from Chloe McArthur, who got it from Brooke Cliveden, who in turn got it from Sister Maureen, one of the two Daughters of Charity who live in a sort of mini-convent attached to the Catholic church. Lydia was supposed to be attending embroidery classes there, but Sister Maureen was adamant that she was not there, and never had been. What is she hiding? Presumably it was something that she didn't want her husband to know about. Go and pay another visit to Lydia Gillette tomorrow, Glyn, and put the frighteners on. There may be more to the grieving widow than meets the eye.'

'And what will you do, sir?"

'I'm going to follow that bottle of peach brandy to its source, beginning with a man called Charles Deacon. I've looked him up, and he seems to be a law-abiding citizen. It's just odd that he should have bought a bottle of very rare brandy when until recently he was living on benefits. Come on, Glyn, let's get out of here!'

* * *

The yellow-brick house in Gladstone Road looked inscrutable to Detective Sergeant Glyn Edwards as it lay bathed in the early autumn sun. A house, perhaps, that held secrets, if its owner had been appallingly done to death. The front garden behind the Victorian brick walls looked unloved, given the minimum care necessary to preserve respectability. All the houses in Gladstone Road were detached, though he could see from the bristle of doorbells that some of them had been converted into flats.

Not this one, though. He rang the lone bell, and the door was opened by Lydia Gillette herself. She was evidently a woman who cared about her appearance, but she looked ravaged with grief, her eyes red-rimmed.

'Oh, it's you,' she said in a lacklustre voice, and preceded him into the bland oatmeal drawing room. A mug of tea stood on a table, beside a plate of Rich Tea biscuits. The tea had gone cold, and there was a milky scum on its surface. Lydia motioned to him to sit down and burst into speech.

'What can I do for you, Sergeant? As I told you and the inspector when you brought me the news that my husband had been murdered with cyanide, I know nothing about my husband's death.' Her voice rattled on nonetheless, as if she couldn't shut off her thoughts. 'His funeral will be this coming Wednesday at All Saints. There will be a reception here, afterwards. Bishop Poindexter will be away, so Canon Murchison will take the service. Louis will be buried in the churchyard. My father will be here, of course, and so will the Lord Mayor . . . Louis was very much esteemed in the community.'

Lydia Gillette began to cry quietly, and Glyn Edwards looked at her. This grief — or was it fear? — seemed not only excessive but unusual: most grieving people were stunned for quite a time after the loss of a loved one, endowed with a kind of desperate courage that saw them successfully through the first raw days. But this was different. Was it grief, or *remorse*? Some lines from a poem came unbidden into his mind: *It is the blight man was born for/ It is Margaret you mourn for.*

'I'm sorry for your loss,' said Glyn. 'At the moment, we are making enquiries in a number of directions, and I'm confident that very shortly now we'll discover the truth of Mr Gillette's death.'

'He knew he was a failure,' said Lydia, 'but never had the courage to admit it. You see, he could always rely on Daddy to get him out of any financial difficulties. I've talked to my solicitor, and he assures me that this house is mine, unencumbered by secret mortgages. I shall stay here. This is where I belong.'

She was an attractive woman, slim and good-looking, in her early fifties. She had spoken unguardedly about her dead husband. Had she grown tired of him? And had she—

Quite suddenly he knew the truth of Lydia's situation: why she had called Jack Prosser — 'an old friend', she had said — rather than going to the gallery herself to see what was amiss. You wouldn't call a friend to run such an errand for you, but you might call a lover. And that potential lover, Jack Prosser, was currently locked up in the basement of Jubilee House. What did *he* get up to on Tuesday evenings?

'Mrs Gillette,' said DS Edwards, and there was an edge of authority in his voice that he reserved for moments such as these, 'the time has come for me to speak plainly, and for you to give me some honest answers. Why did you lie to your husband and friends about where you went on Tuesday evenings? You never went to embroidery classes at the Catholic church. Did your late husband find out? Or did he die not knowing that his wife was deceiving him?'

It was a dangerous thing to say, but it hit its mark. Lydia Gillette rose from the couch, clasping her hands in a kind of agonised despair.

'How did you know? Yes, I betrayed him, and I'll suffer for that for the rest of my life! But can you imagine what it's like for a woman to find that her husband is no longer interested in her? You know what I mean. It has been many months since Louis looked at me in that way, and I grew tired of being rejected.' Her face suffused with pinkness — was it shame or anger? As if reading his thoughts, she met his eyes defiantly. 'What is the point of a marriage without intimacy? I looked for — for solace elsewhere, and that's where I was on those Tuesday evenings. But I shan't tell you who it is that I've been with. That will remain my secret, Detective Sergeant Edwards.'

Glyn thought of the wretched man languishing in the cells at Jubilee House, refusing to speak. Jack Prosser, her childhood friend . . .

'It's as clear as the nose on my face who your new man was, Mrs Gillette. It was your friend Jack Prosser. He's locked up in our cells, refusing to speak for fear of implicating you.' He tried not to let his voice shake at the lie — a little drama was needed to push Lydia to acknowledge the identity of her lover. 'Tell me that I am right, and I will do all that I can to keep your role in all this private. Confess now, and you will be able to visit Jack Prosser, and maybe you'll persuade him to open his mouth.'

Lydia had been turning whiter and whiter as he spoke, but at this point she reddened again and drew herself up, enraged. 'If you think that I would—'

'No, Mrs Gillette, I'm not asking you to rat out your lover or help your husband's killer,' Glyn said hurriedly, not sure exactly where Lydia's loyalties lay but determined not to lose the thread of his argument. 'And I don't think Jack murdered your husband. But he did something . . .' He hesitated, and then went on carefully, 'He did something that has muddied the crime scene, so to speak. He needs to explain his actions, so that we can find your husband's killer. If you do nothing else for Louis, do *this*.'

His final words did the trick. She brushed aside a tear and took a deep breath. Glyn Edwards produced his notebook and a pencil, and Lydia Gillette began to speak.

* * *

Charles Deacon and his wife lived in social housing in Moxton Hill, a northern suburb of Oldminster, where the town petered out into farmland and market gardens. Detective Inspector Paul French brought his car to a halt outside 6 Morrison Road, a semi-detached house with a time-ravaged front garden, used as a parking lot for a motorcycle and side car covered with tarpaulin. Paul French walked up the path and knocked on the door.

'Yes?'

The door had been opened by a pale-faced woman in jogging pants and a black top. Her greying hair was tied back in an untidy ponytail secured by elastic bands.

'Mrs Deacon? I'd like to have a word with your husband, if he's available. I'm Detective Inspector French.'

'You'd better come in, then. Charlie! There's a policeman here to see you.'

Mrs Deacon seemed a defeated sort of woman. She showed no curiosity about why her husband should be visited by a policeman. She simply pointed towards the living room and retreated to the kitchen.

The living room was a nondescript place, the only interesting feature being a brand-new three-piece suite in bulbous leather. Charles Deacon rose from one of the armchairs and shook the inspector's hand. He was wearing a blue pinstriped suit, and what was obviously a brand-new white shirt and striped tie. He was a slight, sandy-haired man, with an irresolute, almost cringing manner, his eyes making an effort to meet those of Paul French but failing to do so. He spoke quietly, and with a refined accent, but his voice was tremulous, and a vein throbbed at his temple.

Paul French had come across all kinds of men in his time, bullies and sneaks, frauds and failures. He looked at Charles Deacon and thought, *This man is an alcoholic, a man born to failure.*

He showed Deacon his warrant card, and Deacon said, 'What can I do for you, Inspector? Please sit down.'

'It's only a small matter, Mr Deacon — something connected to the murder of Louis Gillette, the gallery owner. Nothing involving you directly. Did you purchase a bottle of peach brandy from Mauleverer's Wine Merchants in Carlisle Street recently? A bottle of Lauretier Fils Grande Amber Peach Brandy?'

'Yes, that's right, I did. I paid cash for it, and the man behind the counter put it into a fancy bag for me.'

'Did you buy it for your own consumption?'

There was a pause, and French saw Deacon tense his whole body. At the same time his face flushed with what was evidently vexation.

'No, I bought it on behalf of a — a friend. Why do you want to know this? It's not a crime to buy a bottle of brandy.' His attempt to raise his voice ended in pathetic failure. There was no way in which Charles Deacon could intimidate anyone. He was not the type.

'And who was this friend? You'd better tell me. As you yourself said, it's not a crime to buy a bottle of brandy.'

'It was — it was Manfred Tauber, of Grace Hall. He asked me to buy it for him and gave me the money to do so.'

Suddenly the man seemed to find a reserve of courage. He sat up in his chair, and for the first time looked DI French in the eyes.

'Do you know what it's like to be at the end of your tether, Mr French? Absolutely desperate for money, and with no one to turn to? Mary — my wife — hasn't been well and had to give up her job. I was out of work, with no prospect of getting any, and we were falling into arrears with the rent. I was hopelessly in debt.

'And in desperation I called upon Mr Tauber — I used to be a clerk in his bank, which he sold to NatWest — and begged him to help me. *Begged*. And instead of turning me out, he settled all my debts with a single cheque for three thousand pounds.'

The man's eyes filled with tears.

'Can you imagine that, Mr French? Can you imagine *anyone* being as generous as that? Mr Tauber gave me back my life. So when he asked me to run a little errand for him, I was off like a shot. He's going to find me different small jobs to do for him, until I'm fit enough to get back into work. I'm — I'm an alcoholic, Inspector, but Mr Tauber's arranged for me to attend AA meetings in town. There's nothing I wouldn't do for him.'

'And did you take the bottle of peach brandy up to him at Grace Hall?'

'Yes. I saw Mr Williams, the house manager, and handed it to him. He gave me a fiver, and I came back here.'

Paul French stood up and treated Deacon to a disarming smile.

'Well, thank you, Mr Deacon, you've been most helpful. I'm sorry to hear that you've had difficulties, and I wish you all the best for the future. I'll see myself out.'

He lingered in the hall, and heard Mrs Deacon say, 'You fool! You couldn't even keep Mr Tauber's name out of this.'

'How was I to know that someone in the shop would recognise me?'

'You should've been more careful. One little job he asked you to do, and you couldn't even get that right!'

* * *

It took longer than he'd have liked for Paul French to be buzzed through the large, ornate gates of Grace Hall. As he drove up the winding driveway he thought back to the sorry house that Charles Deacon lived in, and the gratitude bubbling over in the unhappy man when he'd told him about Tauber paying off his debts. Like the fawning servant of the lord of the manor, bought and paid for. Was it really just the one little job that Deacon had done for Tauber?

A smart-looking fellow answered the door and inspected his warrant card, then said, 'I'm John Williams, the house manager here, Inspector. How can I help you?'

Paul French thought, *Not a hair out of place, and the smile just wide enough to disarm the unwary. I don't trust you, my friend!*

'I wonder whether you can confirm that a man called Charles Deacon bought a bottle of peach brandy for Mr

Manfred Tauber, and brought it up here, to Grace Hall? My question's part of an ongoing inquiry, you'll understand.'

'Peach brandy? Yes, that was the Lauretier Fils Grande Amber. We keep a single bottle of that particular brandy in the cellar here. Mr Tauber has an extensive wine cellar, and a large selection of spirits, though he's essentially a wine-drinking man.'

'Can you recall the date when Mr Deacon bought the brandy?'

'The date? Well, it would have been the eleventh. It's not my place to ask questions, Inspector, but I'm intrigued to know why you should be so interested in the contents of Mr Tauber's cellar. Would you care to look around?'

'Yes, I would, Mr Williams. Thank you very much.'

The cellars were extensive, with vaulted ceilings dating from the fourteenth century. Williams explained that there had been an earlier house on the site before the great Tudor mansion was built. Rack after rack held venerable cobwebby bottles of rare vintages.

'Here are the brandies, Inspector. All sorts of delights here — Louis XVI, and there's the Remy Martin Louis XIII — we've four bottles of that. And there's the Lauretier Fils Grande Amber that Deacon bought for us.' Williams opened a notebook standing on one of the racks and flicked through the pages. 'Here's the entry, Inspector: "Tuesday, 11 September. Lauretier Fils Grande Amber. Lodged in rack fourteen.".'

So much for that, thought DI French. A dead end? Perhaps.

* * *

At eleven o'clock on the morning of Monday, 24 September, DS Edwards switched on the tape recorder in the interview room at Jubilee House, and Jack Prosser began to make his confession.

'On the evening of Friday, 14 September, Lydia Gillette called me at my apartment in Bankside Flats, saying that she was worried, as her husband, Louis, had not returned home from the Rembrandt Gallery. She asked me to drive into town to check that he was all right. I described what happened when I got to the Arcade in my previous statement to the police.'

DI French: 'We need to hear that again, for the purposes of this statement.'

'When I arrived at the gallery, I rang the bell, and I was admitted by the night watchman. The Arcade was still lit up, though some of the shops were in darkness. The watchman told me that Mr Gillette was still in the gallery. He left me, and I entered the premises of the Rembrandt Gallery. I went through to the inner room, where Louis Gillette had his office, and saw that he was lying dead across his desk.

'There was a strong smell of peaches and alcohol in the room, and I saw that there was an empty brandy glass lying on its side on the table. Between Gillette's hands was a piece of paper, upon which he had written: "I cannot face my creditors. Lydia must not be dragged down by me."'

DS Edwards: 'So the statement that you made to me that night was a lie. Why did you lie, Mr Prosser?'

'When I saw that Gillette had committed suicide, I was horrified, but I was intensely angry, too. How could he have done such a thing? How would Lydia bear the disgrace of being the widow of a suicide!'

'That is a very unusual motivation for tampering with a crime scene in this day and age, Mr Prosser.'

'Perhaps, if you didn't know Lydia. I've known her all my life. She never recovered from her mother's death. People will tell you that her death was an unfortunate accident, but the truth of it is that Lydia's mother attempted suicide. She regretted her action but caught septicaemia as a result of her injuries and died not long after.'

'Even so . . .'

'Believe me, Sergeant, if Louis had committed suicide it would have been too heavy a blow for Lydia. You know, now, that I love Lydia — I've loved her since we were teens together, before ever Gillette came on the scene. I couldn't bring him back to life, but I could make his death look like murder. I picked up the glass and put it in the pocket of my overcoat. I removed the suicide note, too. Much later that morning, after I'd been to see Lydia, I ground the wineglass to pieces in the street, and scraped it with my shoe down a grid. I set fire to the suicide note, and it burnt to ashes.'

DS Edwards: 'Describe the note. Was it in Louis Gillette's handwriting?'

'No, it was typewritten, and Louis had not signed it.'

DI French: 'Did you do anything else to the room, or the body? You must tell us everything.'

'I just stood there, looking at him lying dead, and I was sorry he'd been driven to kill himself. I'll never forget that moment. Never. I'm glad it's over. The safe was open, but there was nothing in it. I didn't murder Louis. He was dead when I got there.'

DI French spoke into the recorder: 'Interview concluded at eleven thirty-two a.m.'

'We believe you when you say that you didn't murder Louis Gillette,' he said, 'but you have committed grave misdemeanours: tampering with evidence and lying to the police. I'm going to release you on police bail, but you will certainly face charges. You must not leave Oldminster, and you must show yourself here every day until further notice.'

Paul French looked at Jack Prosser, and saw a man racked with guilt and remorse, but he could feel no pity for him. He was the third side in an eternal triangle, a man who'd shown little regard for the law. He was self-regarding, self-centred, and there were crimes and misdemeanours for which he would have to pay.

'You can go,' said DI French.

* * *

Debbie, the manageress and chief stylist at Barry's Stylists, a bustling salon off Northumberland Street in Newcastle city centre, enthused about Donald Wainwright.

'A very nice man, he is, Ms McArthur,' she said, 'a real gentleman, but with no side on him, if you know what I mean. And he's a friend of yours? Fancy that!'

Barry's Stylists was a bright, attractive place, staffed by four chatty hairstylists, who that Monday afternoon were all fully occupied with clients. Debbie, a cheerful woman in her thirties, had taken Chloe into her minuscule office behind a bead curtain at the back of the shop. They were drinking coffee from mugs. Chloe thought of the Blue Mountain coffee at home and suppressed a sigh. She didn't like the way Debbie was eyeing her hair, as if she was itching to take her scissors to it.

'And there's another salon, isn't there, belonging to the same owner?'

'Yes, that's right. Brenda's Hair Heaven, just off Gallowgate, across town. It's quite nice, Mrs McArthur, but not as nice as Barry's!'

'The present owner—'

'Yes, Jacob Solomon. He's what they call a property developer, but he's not a stylist or anything like that. He's selling off a couple of businesses like this because he wants to invest in a new development that's going up in Gateshead. He comes in here every quarter. A very nice man, well thought of here in Newcastle.'

'Have you seen anything of Donald Wainwright recently? Now that I'm here, I'd like to pay him a visit. If he's really set his heart on buying these two salons, I shan't stand in his way. Unfortunately, I don't know his address in Newcastle.'

'We've not heard from him recently,' said Debbie. 'I expect that's because he's been dealing with Mr Solomon directly. I don't know. But if you want to visit him, I can give you his address. It's number six, Leopold Terrace, just opposite St James's Park. You can get a bus out there, or you might like to take a taxi. Now, before you go, I was just admiring your lovely hair — have you been thinking of getting it cut recently?'

* * *

Number 6 Leopold Terrace was a nondescript house of the 'two up, two down' variety in the shadow of Newcastle United's ground. It looked empty and neglected, the last kind of house that Louis Gillette would have chosen to live in. But then, it could only ever have been an item in his programme of changing himself into 'Donald Wainwright', and disappearing abroad, to live on the proceeds of his grand theft from his wealthy father-in-law.

Had Louis been serious about buying the two hairdressing salons? Maybe. After all, 'Donald Wainwright' was as pure as the driven snow, because he was a man without a history. She'd seen a programme on TV about laundering money through small businesses like hairdressers and garages, though she'd have to talk to an accountant to understand how it was done.

The ninety thousand pounds, and available money to buy the hairdressing businesses, had all come from his grand swindle against Simon Bolt. Where was the rest? She was becoming almost fearful of what she might expose to the light of day.

Louis Gillette and 'Donald Wainwright' were both dead and buried. Why had she come out here? She had no way of getting into the house. Feeling rather frustrated, she pushed the front door, and it swung open. Without hesitation, she stepped into the narrow hall. There were a number of letters on the floor, most of them junk mail by the sight of it. The house smelt close and stale, and when she quickly surveyed the rooms on the ground floor, she saw that it was unfurnished. Mounting the uncarpeted stairs, she entered the back bedroom, which was minimally furnished with a camp bed and a bedside table. Inside the drawer she found two passports, one British and one French. Each contained the name of 'Donald Wainwright'. Each carried a photograph of Louis Gillette.

It was much later that Chloe McArthur realised consciously that she had walked into a trap, but even in this moment something made her twitchy. What a fool she had been not to smell a rat when she'd found the front door invitingly open! There was no time to shrink away, nowhere to hide. There came a mad rush of heavy boots on the stairs and in seconds she had been seized by a huge, spitting, cursing brute of a man, who dragged her out onto the landing, and threw her down the stairs. Stunned and terrified, she lay in agony while the brute, a man with huge biceps and a tattooed face, stood over her. As she lapsed into unconsciousness, she heard the man say, 'Back off. You're not in our league. You're playing a losing game.'

6. THE HOUSE IN LEOPOLD TERRACE

The funeral of Louis Gillette was held at All Saints, a Victorian Gothic church a few streets away from the dead man's house in Gladstone Road. That Wednesday morning was dry, but scudding clouds threatened rain later. DI French and DS Edwards sat in one of the back pews, listening to a rather amorphous, low-key piece of music designed by the organist to keep the mourners content until the arrival of the coffin.

The doors of the church opened, and the procession entered, led by Canon Murchison, deputising for Bishop Poindexter. Glyn Edwards glanced at the coffin, its brass handles gleaming, and with a wreath of lilies on the lid, and thought of the abused and battered body lying there at rest.

I am the resurrection and the life, saith the Lord: he that believeth in me, though he were dead, yet shall he live . . .

Lydia followed, supported by her father, who looked suitably grim; he had had no love for his son-in-law, but objected strongly to his being murdered: things like that didn't happen to the Bolts.

Glyn Edwards watched as the coffin was placed on the catafalque, and the mourners eased themselves into the front pews. All Lydia's friends from the Cathedral Ladies' Guild were there: Claudia Hurst, the librarian at the Bishop's palace;

Felicity Campbell; some other ladies and two men whom he didn't recognise; and Chloe McArthur, who was no stranger to Jubilee House. Poor Chloe had rather a nasty-looking cut on her head. He wondered whether they all knew by now that Lydia had been unfaithful to Louis? The building of All Saints had been bankrolled by a staunchly Protestant stockbroker in 1855, and it was he who had insisted that the altar be flanked with two stone tablets bearing the ten commandments. Would Lydia read her own reproach in the words of the Seventh: *Thou shalt not commit adultery?*

There were two hymns, and a brief address from the Canon, but no long eulogy from one of the dead man's relatives or friends. After half an hour, everybody moved out into the churchyard for the committal. The rain had held off, but it was still a dull and cheerless morning. The two detectives stood discreetly beside a tall monument to a defunct Victorian worthy, a monument topped by the figure of a weeping angel.

They saw how Simon Bolt supported his daughter physically as she stood at the graveside. She was dressed in black, with a widow's black veil, and seemed to have shrunk in stature since Edwards had last seen her. She shuddered as she threw the customary handful of soil on the coffin and was enfolded in her father's bear-like embrace. The committal was soon over, and the mourners walked slowly back to the waiting cars.

'There he is,' said DI French.

Jack Prosser was standing some way off by a line of trees flanking the far side of the graveyard. It was clear that he, like them, had not wanted to be seen, and little wonder, thought Glyn, considering the indignity to which he had subjected the dead man. Why had he come? Was it remorse? Or was it to see whether Lydia Gillette was all right? She was free to marry her childhood sweetheart now, if she wished. But maybe the scales had fallen from her eyes, maybe she realised that she had nothing to gain by associating with that man. Perhaps her father, a powerful, wealthy entrepreneur, would take her back to London with him, where she could forget all about Jack Prosser.

* * *

The next day, Noel Greenspan drove his battered Ford Mondeo to the central train station, where he was to meet his and Chloe's friend and occasional colleague Lance Middleton, QC, who had been once again tempted to leave his bachelor's chambers in Lincoln's Inn by the prospect of sampling one of Chloe McArthur's cordon bleu meals.

With much puffing and inconsequential chatter, he and his luggage were fitted into the car, and Noel drove them to Wellington Square. It was here, in rather shabby-genteel rows of Georgian houses facing each other across a communal garden, that Noel and Chloe both lived, each with an apartment on opposite sides of the square. Noel drove round the square to what he called 'Chloe's side' and extricated their stout friend and his luggage from the Mondeo.

It was just after four o'clock, too late for lunch and too early for dinner, but Chloe's gas-fired Aga was humming away when they entered her apartment, and the air was full of enticing smells which were very pleasing to their gourmet guest.

'Dear Chloe!' he cried, lowering his bulk into one of the kitchen chairs, 'whenever I come here, I find a marriage of true minds! Why must everybody enslave themselves to miserable diets, when God had given us of His plenty, each beast of the field, the fish of the sea, and so on? What are you cooking for us, Chloe?'

'This is a meal for all times and seasons,' said Chloe, 'a compromise between a very late lunch and a very early dinner. We'll start with a light consommé, followed by grilled sirloin of beef, served with mushrooms, tomatoes and battered onions, with a seasonal salad, which is not compulsory — I know you're not very keen on leaves and things like that.'

'So must they dine in the halls of Heaven', said Lance. 'Whenever I come here, I feel that I am coming home. Any pudding?'

'Baked apple and raisin cheesecake. And there's one of Sainsbury's Choice Merlots to accompany it. All will be ready in about fifteen minutes' time.' She brushed her hair back from her face as she spoke.

Lance peered at her closely. 'Wherever did you get that nasty cut on your head?'

'I had a whole funeral to get through of people asking me that yesterday,' Chloe said, chopping mushrooms vigorously. 'I'm rather embarrassed to say it was from falling down the stairs. No, not here,' she went on, 'it was in Newcastle, on a job, on Monday.'

'She was pushed down the stairs in an abandoned house, Lance,' Noel said fretfully. 'She could have been killed.'

'Nonsense. I was being warned off. It was silly of me.'

'Silly of you to be attacked?'

'No, I mean . . .' She put down the knife. 'I kept seeing this unassuming little man wherever I went in Newcastle. He was on the same train as me going up. And then he was looking in an estate agent's window in Gateshead. It seemed coincidental at the time, till I was attacked.'

'By the unassuming little man?'

'Not him, but I think the shadow must have called in someone more intimidating when he saw I was alone. There was no chance of being killed, Noel — I think he meant to frighten me but the stairs were rather narrow and I ended up going down them.'

Lance looked between the two of them, aware suddenly that this was an argument that must have been going on for some time. 'Is this to do with the question you wanted to ask me, Chloe?'

'I want to finish the cooking in peace. Lance, you must go into the sitting room with Noel, and hear why we want to consult you.'

The two men left Chloe to finish her work in the kitchen, which doubled as a dining room, and settled themselves in the sitting room, where a professional designer had given the spacious Regency room a renewed elegance and simplicity by the careful use of silvered wallpapers and antique mirrors. All the furniture, culled from various antique shops in Chichester and elsewhere, fitted the room perfectly. Noel motioned to Lance to settle himself for a while in one of two brocade-covered sofas.

'She is okay, really,' said Noel, 'just a bit shaken, and we have to watch her for any signs of delayed concussion for a couple of weeks. But to explain it all, I should go back a bit. I want you to set aside your baroque nonsense and verbal onslaughts while I tell you the tragic story of Louis Gillette, his wife Lydia, and her boyfriend, Jack Prosser. Gillette was murdered, or so it would seem, but this story involves a hidden trail of money, including a small fortune apparently spirited away by Louis Gillette before he met his death. Chloe and I want to go after the money and see where it leads. We need your knowledge of the City though — the clues are too sparse for us as they stand.'

'Ah! That sounds very interesting. This "small fortune" — how much was it?'

'A million pounds. Gillette managed to swindle his father-in-law of it, apparently without him noticing that it had gone. His father-in-law is an entrepreneur called Simon Bolt.'

'Well, well, this really is interesting. Simon Bolt is not unknown to the various, er — bodies that I sometimes work for. Yes, Simon Bolt's a good start.'

'There's another mystery closely allied to the death of Louis Gillette, also involving a money-trail. Chloe has printed a set of photographs of various documents that she found in a secret drawer in Louis Gillette's desk. But here's Chloe to summon us to the table. As soon as the inner man is satisfied, we'll produce those photographs, and see what they suggest to you.'

When the meal was over, and the percolator containing Blue Mountain coffee was bubbling away, Chloe and Noel cleared the table, and Chloe produced the photographs that she had taken of the secret cache in Louis Gillette's desk.

Lance Middleton had thrown off all his skittishness and gave his full and serious attention to the photographs, examining them closely with the aid of a hand lens.

'This letter from his landlords — Oldshire Estates — is straightforward enough. A demand for payment from what I assume is a reputable letting agency?'

'It is,' said Noel. 'They're a long-established firm, with headquarters here, in Newgate Street.'

'Hm . . . Well, Lydia Gillette will need to settle the bill or give up the gallery. As the relict, she is heir-at-law to all of her husband's estate in money, goods and chattels.'

'I believe she's going to pay what's owing, and probably give up the gallery when the lease is up,' Chloe said. 'I've shared all these details with her too, though they mean little to her in her current state.'

'Now, this letter from Hollingworth, the art expert, sets some alarm bells ringing. Ninety thousand pounds is a goodly sum, but you notice that exclamation mark? "Ha, ha! Silly me!", it says. It suggests that Louis Gillette was not too worried about losing such a large sum to a dealer in copies of genuine art works. Why? Because he had plenty of money stashed away elsewhere. Or was the loss no loss at all?'

'What do you mean? He'd swindled his father-in-law out of a million pounds,' said Chloe. 'I was present when Simon Bolt told Lydia about that. His financial advisor had apparently found out only recently.'

'Exactly, Chloe. So we need to ask this question: how was a failing gallery owner clever enough to fool such a man as Simon Bolt? I don't know who his financial advisor is, but he'll be one of the best in his profession if Bolt uses him. Louis Gillette must have had help in engineering that swindle.'

Lance Middleton folded his hands together as though in prayer. He looked profoundly uneasy.

'I don't like the smell of all this,' he said at last. 'My work in the Department of Justice has made me aware of this kind of fraud, and there's more to it than an individual villain swindling a rich dupe of his money. This fake art trick smells familiar, though — I've come across it before in a case I worked on a few months ago. I think I know who sold Louis Gillette the fake Giotto. It's a man called Samuel Harker, and he's one of a ring of front men for a money-laundering cartel, operating here and in Europe. When I said the loss wasn't really a loss, that's what I was talking about.'

'You mean Louis bought the painting as a front?'

'That's right — you don't pay tax on business losses. But we can't be sure without talking to Harker.'

'I'll pay him a visit,' said Chloe. 'What's his address?'

'If it's all the same to you, Chloe, I'd like to be the one who questions him. I don't want all my clients clamming up on me when they see I'm working with private investigators — makes it devilishly hard to defend someone when you don't have the facts. There is someone else we should talk to in London — a forensic accountant who does a good deal of work for the government. I rather think she started off in the secret service, but that's just a suspicion of mine. Could you pay her a visit? She'll know all about Samuel Harker, and she'll answer your questions as a private investigator. Have you a photograph of Louis Gillette? It would help if I knew what he looked like.'

Chloe took a newspaper cutting from a drawer and gave it to Lance. 'This was taken recently at a Town Hall reception in aid of the Red Cross,' she said. 'That's Louis Gillette, there. It's a very good likeness.'

'Thank you. Well, it's time that I was gone. I must see if I can catch a late train back to London.'

This was part of an ongoing fiction, in which they all played a part. It always ended in the same way.

'Nonsense,' said Noel. 'You must stay the night with me and return to London by a decent train tomorrow. And Chloe can travel up with you.' It had not gone unnoticed that Lance had arrived with an overnight bag as well as an ample briefcase.

The two men left Chloe and made their way round to Noel's side of Wellington Square, where Lance Middleton would stay the night.

* * *

Samuel Harker's art gallery was hidden away in a little cobbled lane off Victoria Street, in the shadow of the great red-brick campanile of Westminster Cathedral. The premises were old, and to Lance Middleton's eye looked ripe for demolition. He climbed the three worn steps and pushed open the door, setting a little bell jingling. It was dark inside, and the walls were covered by large classical paintings in elaborate frames.

Samuel Harker, a pale-faced man in his forties with an arthritic stoop, emerged from the dim recesses of the shop, to see who had disturbed the peace and quiet of his premises.

'Good morning! How may I help you?' he said, and then, recognising his visitor, he drew in his breath with a little hiss of either apprehension or vexation.

'Lance Middleton, QC,' he said. 'We don't often see you in Pecan Lane. Have you come to buy a picture? I've got an authentic seventeenth-century portrait of Judge Jeffreys. That would look very nice in your chambers in Lincoln's Inn.'

'Well, Mr Harker,' said Lance, 'I've not come to buy anything, I'm afraid, but I did want to talk to you about a painting that you sold to Louis Gillette — supposedly a Giotto, but it turned out to be a fake. It was you who sold it to him, wasn't it? I have ways of finding out these things through Her Majesty's Revenue and Customs — you might as well tell me.'

'Why deny it?' said Samuel Harker, smiling. 'Yes, I sold it to poor Louis Gillette. I asked for ninety thousand, and he transferred the money to me immediately. But the Giotto turned out to be a fake. He got an expert in to look at it, and he proved it to be a forgery. Very embarrassing. He brought it back here, and I said that I would give him his money back, but that he'd have to wait a week or so, as the money had been paid away to meet other liabilities. But now he's dead, well . . . I need to take legal advice, as you'll well realise.'

A well-rehearsed story. You've got an answer for everything, my friend, thought Lance.

'What happened to the fake Giotto?'

'It's here, in the back room. Obviously, I can't put it on show until it's been investigated by the insurers. I bought it in good faith on my annual visit to Florence — seventy thousand I paid for it. So we all lost out, you see. These things do happen. Would you like to buy it, as a curiosity? I'll take three hundred for it, though you'd have to wait for the painting. Insurers, you know.'

'Well, no thank you, Mr Harker,' said Lance, 'though it's very kind of you to make the offer. You've been very helpful. I'm looking into a few things for the relict, Mrs Lydia Gillette. As you can imagine, she's distraught at losing her husband in that way, and needs a legal friend to see that all goes well with probate, and so on.'

'We live in terrible times, Mr Middleton. "Death cancels all debts," they say. But I'm not so sure about that.'

Lance Middleton left the gallery, noting that Mr Harker had a new Jaguar XE2 parked in the alley beside the premises. Harker followed him out and stood at the front door at the top of the steps, smiling as he walked away.

* * *

Sarah Townsend, the forensic accountant Lance had recommended, worked in a cramped set of rooms in a nondescript office block overlooking St James's Park. She sat at a plain wooden table, surrounded by tall, green metal filing cabinets. On the table was a rather clunky-looking computer, an antique-style telephone and a half-eaten cheese sandwich.

She was dressed in cropped pinstripe trousers, silk shirt and red loafers.

'If you get too near to Samuel Harker, Chloe,' said Sarah Townsend, 'you'll get your fingers burnt. He's a genuine art dealer, and from what I have heard, is much better at his job than Louis Gillette ever was. He's also a money launderer, though he's good at covering his tracks, and he specialises in building up private fortunes abroad for people who want to avoid paying tax — any kind of tax, either here, or abroad.'

'How does he do that?'

'He'll sell you a painting — a genuine item or a copy as the mood takes him — for a certain sum agreed between you, say ninety thousand pounds, which is the sum you mentioned in connection with his deal with Louis Gillette. The painting is obtained abroad, and your ninety thousand pounds is lodged in a foreign bank. Some weeks later, a number of bills are paid from that account, amounting to, say, nine thousand pounds. Those bills merely disguise Harker's fee for laundering your ninety thousand, which will have been transmuted for your convenience into euros or dollars. He's moved vaster sums than that, I'm sure of it, but it's hard to prove it.'

Chloe thought of the exclamation mark written on the letter from Mr Hollingworth: *I paid £90,000 for it!* It had not been a note of complaint, but a cry of triumph.

'So Louis Gillette was as big a rogue as Samuel Harker.'

'Not quite, Chloe. Harker is a big-time player. Gillette was just one of his customers. And we have to remember that Louis Gillette is dead. Murdered.'

'Louis swindled his father-in-law of a million pounds. He couldn't have done that alone. I don't think he was clever enough.'

'He could well have used Harker again, but with a sum like that, he would have needed the services of a crooked accountant or auditor. Harker has quite a network of shady types.'

'Why don't the authorities close him down, send him to jail?'

'I can't be sure, because I'm out of the loop nowadays, but I'd say he's of much greater use to somebody when he's at large.'

'So they just let him and all his rich friends get away with fleecing the rest of us?'

Sarah Townsend shifted in her chair and bit her lip.

'There's more to it than that,' she said. 'There are ramifications . . . It's not just doing shady deals for folk like Louis Gillette. There are other, secret deals on an international scale, involving purchase of arms for insurrectionists . . . Sabotage of installations, funding of arms traders . . . Someone like Harker is useful because he is supposedly under the radar. He can provide leads when other methods fail. Do you understand?'

'I think so,' said Chloe slowly.

'I can't say too much, Chloe, but I'm warning you to be very careful. Perhaps you need to ask yourself a different set of questions about the death of Louis Gillette.'

* * *

Some of the most exciting gastronomic experiences in London are hidden in unusual places — under railway arches, at the tops of skyscrapers, and in this case on a deserted street in Waterloo, down a steep and rather narrow set of steps. Lance Middleton was hovering uncertainly at the top of the restaurant steps. He was looking forward to a pleasant brunch with Chloe before she caught the train back home — but why was she taking so long with Sarah Townsend? Should he have gone with her as her protector, after her unpleasant experience in the Newcastle terrace?

He was just taking out his phone to call her when he spotted something else that made him even more nervous: a stranger was staring at him rather too fixedly. Hadn't he seen the same stranger outside Chloe's house yesterday? Was this the unassuming-looking man whom Chloe had seen on her journey to Newcastle?

As if in confirmation, a tattooed arm snaked around his neck from behind and began to choke the life out of him. 'I've told you lot before, back off,' snarled a gruff voice. 'Next time you won't be getting up again.'

Lance gasped for breath and tried to pull himself free, but it was no use. Just as he started to lose consciousness, he heard a welcome sound: shouts from the street, and the sound of a siren. The grip on his neck was released, and his attacker sent him with a push tumbling down the stairs.

7. VIRGIN AND CHILD WITH PRIMROSE

'He's in St Thomas's Hospital. Badly bruised and battered, but with no vital organs compromised.'

Assembled that afternoon were DI French, DS Edwards, Noel Greenspan and Chloe McArthur. Chloe, having seen Lance in hospital before she'd caught the fast train home for the conference, was tearful. Noel was in the mood to take all the blame.

'It's my fault, Paul,' he said, 'I should have realised that we weren't dealing with amateurs. I should have alerted you to what was going on.'

'Yes, you should have. We're all on speaking terms, here — why didn't you tell us about the attack in Newcastle, Chloe? The police there weren't to know it was relevant to Oldshire Police, but you should have done.'

'I'm sorry, Paul. I suppose I was embarrassed about walking into a trap.'

'It's nothing to be ashamed of — I've walked into plenty of scrapes myself. Sometimes that's the way an investigation goes. But from now on, let's keep each other informed about what's going on. From what you've told us, it sounds like you and Lance were both being warned off. In this case, the thug was choking him, then panicked when he was seen and pushed Lance away. This was never intended to be a fatal attack.

'Chloe, I'd like you to talk to our artist so that we can get together an E-FIT of the man who you said was following you in Newcastle, and also of the thug who attacked you.'

'Well, I'll do my best with the second,' she said bravely. 'He came from behind, and I was barely able to see when he loomed over me. But I've been trying to get a CCTV image from the train company of the man who was tailing me — you might be able to speed things up on that front.'

'Very well. In the meantime, I'm sending DS Edwards out to interview Lydia Gillette once again, and to tell her the whole story of her husband's double life. From what I gather, she seems to regard herself as the guilty party because of her adultery with that fellow Prosser, but I'm beginning to think that she's a woman more sinned against than sinning. And I want you to go with him, since you've been working for her — Lydia has been a bit short-tempered with us so far. Glyn, have you anything you want to add?'

'Yes, sir, I think we need to be quite clear in our minds what we are investigating: the murder of Louis Gillette. Set aside for a minute — with apologies, Chloe — the money and the warnings. The facts are: Jack Prosser found and destroyed a glass and a typewritten suicide note, but we know it was murder because the brandy bottle containing the cyanide wasn't at the scene.'

'That's true,' said DI French. 'And we know that just before Louis Gillette was murdered, a thickset man carrying a holdall was seen going into the Rembrandt Gallery. Glyn and I are both convinced that that man was the murderer. For murder it was, we've no doubt about that. Motive? We've no real idea at the moment, beyond guesses. Glyn?'

'Parallel to the murder, sir, we have this business of the money — the swindling of Simon Bolt, Lydia Gillette's father; the attempts by Louis Gillette to set up a new identify and abandon his life in Oldshire. Noel and Chloe have done some good work on that front. They seem to understand all this talk of losses and laundering better than I do, too. I'm more interested in the murder than the money.'

'And yet the money could lead to the motive, and so to the killer,' said DI French. 'Don't forget that, Glyn. Let's all go down to the canteen and get some coffee and biscuits. I'm due to see Superintendent Philpot in half an hour, to update him on what's going on. Noel, you can stay here at Jubilee House and read Jack Prosser's confession, if you like. That's all for today, I think.'

* * *

'So he was going to leave me,' said Lydia Gillette. Chloe McArthur looked at her friend, and thought, *She seems relieved. That's because she no longer needs to bear the whole burden of guilt for the slow extinction of her marriage to Louis.*

'Thank you for telling me all this, Sergeant Edwards. And there was a secret drawer in his desk . . . You should have told me, Chloe.'

'I'm sorry, Lydia — I did tell you about the contents, remember? You were so upset that day—'

'Oh, it doesn't matter now. He . . . Louis' parents were long dead, and I was all that he had. But our marriage was dead, too — I don't care who knows about it, now. He was never unfaithful to me, as far as I know. That's because he was essentially a loner. He didn't need anybody. He married because that's the thing one is meant to do, but his heart belonged to that wretched gallery with its second-rate exhibits. No wonder I began to look elsewhere . . .'

Lydia began to cry very quietly. The morning sun streamed in through the drawing-room windows of the house in Gladstone Road, betraying the fact that the room had not been properly dusted for some time.

'Mrs Gillette,' said DS Edwards, 'I want you to understand that you have committed no crime in the eyes of the law. I have brought a search warrant with me, so that I can take away the contents of that secret drawer. You can accompany me if you wish.'

Lydia seemed not to hear.

'I would have let a decent interval elapse before I married Jack Prosser. I should have married him when I was a girl, but Louis was so handsome and debonair, a cultured man, whereas Jack . . . Daddy warned me not to marry Louis. He said he was weak. And now . . . You say that Jack tampered with the crime scene? What does that mean? What did he do? Was it something that I could forgive?' She paused and looked at Chloe. 'I did as you suggested and checked Louis's will. He left just about everything to me, and this house was never re-mortgaged.'

Chloe balked. *She's contemplating a future life with Jack.* She thought. *Should I say something more?* To do so might ruin their friendship, but she couldn't say nothing. Lydia deserved better than Jack Prosser.

Before she could say anything, Glyn spoke up. 'Jack Prosser found your husband dead and thought that he had committed suicide. So, to save you from the disgrace of having a husband who took his own life, he destroyed the note and the glass your husband had drunk from. Then he lost his nerve and tried to skip town. It's not my place to comment on the morality or otherwise of Jack Prosser's action.'

Lydia had gone very pale. Chloe got up from her chair and joined her on the settee.

'I heard from your father the other day. He's saying you won't take up his invitation to stay in London with him,' she said. 'Wouldn't it be a good idea? To take a break from Oldminster?'

'But I belong here!' Lydia cried. 'I've lived here since I was a child. All my friends are here. Oh, leave me alone, both of you. Finish your snooping upstairs and go!'

* * *

Later that afternoon Noel Greenspan received a call from St Thomas's Hospital in London. It was from a charge nurse, informing him that Lance Middleton was feeling much better, but that he would have to stay in hospital for observation.

'He's going to be all right, is he, Nurse?'

'Oh, yes. We've had far worse on this ward.'

'Is he behaving himself? He's a bit of a "larger than life" kind of man, fond of his own voice.' He heard the nurse laugh.

'He doesn't think much of the food and wants to tell the cooks how to make all kinds of fancy French dishes! Would you like to speak to him?'

Lance Middleton's voice was more subdued than usual, but it was clear that the attack had in no way broken his spirit. But it was time to thank him for his services and call a halt to his part in the investigation.

'I blame myself, Lance, for letting you loose in the way I did. I should have arranged a "shadow" to keep you in sight. Anyway, you'll want to bow out now—'

There came an indignant splutter through the line.

'"Bow out?" No way am I bowing out. I saw that rogue Samuel Harker, and we bandied words together. I could see from the way he looked at me that he'd guessed I knew what his little game was. Money laundering on a vast scale. And here's another interesting thing — you talked about "shadows". I'm convinced now that Chloe and I were followed from Oldminster by the same person who followed Chloe to Newcastle. Just before I was attacked I saw a weedy, nondescript type of man staring fixedly at me. When the thug started choking the life out of me he looked horrified and ran away.'

'A weedy man?'

'Yes. A sort of shabby, nondescript type of man, the type of man you find propping up a bar and moaning about the government.

'When they've done with me here, I'm going after the big money. I'm going after Simon Bolt's missing million, and I know where to start. We had lasagne for tea yesterday. It was — it was a crime against cuisine. I offered to give the cook a recipe of my own — well, not my own, but one concocted by my treasure of a restaurateur in London. What? Time's up, nurse? Why are you sticking something in my ear? Oh, it's a thermometer. Years ago, you folk stuck things like that in a fellow's mouth. And it was all in Fahrenheit then, so you knew what they were talking about. Sit up? I am sitting up . . .'

The nurse's voice came down the line. She sounded thoroughly amused.

'I think you can guess what progress Mr Middleton's making,' she said. 'But for the moment, he's about to engage in a battle with me — a battle that he won't win!'

* * *

Not long after his return from Oldminster, Simon Bolt looked out of the morning-room window of his grand house in an exclusive street off Cheyne Walk, and thought, *Who's taking a delivery this time of day?* A foreign van, by the looks of it. Daladier Frères, Lyon. French, then.

Lydia had refused to come to London with him. More fool she! The break would have done her good — and London was a better place for moving on and reinventing yourself than Oldminster, any day. She'd come round in the end, when common sense prevailed. But, then again, the people in that part of the country were genuine. Those friends of Lydia's were a good lot. They weren't in it for the money.

Hello, he thought, *the driver from that van's coming up the front path.* He was a smart-looking fellow in a light blue uniform. The doorbell rang, and in a few moments Grove, the butler, came into the room. He was holding a sheet of paper.

'Sir,' he said, 'there's a man at the door who's delivering a picture you ordered. He wants a signature to show that you've received it.'

'Couldn't you have signed for it, Grove? What picture? Perhaps it's something those interior designers bought for the old billiards room. Here, let me sign for it. Then you can have the man take it through.'

He took the sheet of paper from Grove and prepared to sign it. It was a combined delivery note and invoice, headed Gebruder Klapwijk Frères, Antwerp. Three lines in French, English and Dutch, said that they were forwarding agents.

Painting. Virgin and Child with Primrose. Tintoretto, 1525.
£90,000. Paid with thanks.

That sum struck a chord. Lydia had told him about the ninety thousand pounds and the fake Giotto. Was this another of Louis's purchases? But why had it come here?

They went out into the front court, and watched as the driver, now assisted by another uniformed man, wheeled a tall wooden crate across the forecourt. With much heaving and sighing they brought the crate into the wide hall. It was well and professionally packed. Whatever villainy Louis Gillette had been up to, it was clear that neither the carrier nor the forwarding agent had anything to do with it.

'Can you men undo this thing?' asked Simon Bolt. At the same time, he produced two twenty-pound notes from his wallet. The two men set to with a will, and soon they had removed all the protective wrappings and plywood stiffeners to reveal a beautiful painting that looked centuries old. Framed by a crumbling arch, the Virgin sat with her child on a bank of flowers. She was holding a primrose in one hand. In the distance, a small turreted castle stood on a hill, and above it, a crescent moon shone in an azure sky.

'What do you think of it, Grove?'

'Well, sir, it's very beautiful, and all that, but I don't think it's quite your style of thing. Very Catholic, you know. Not the kind of thing to put in a billiards room.'

'Do you think it's genuine?'

'Well, sir, there is rather a strong smell of paint, which you wouldn't really expect from an antique painting.' Grove touched one corner gingerly with a finger. 'And as you can see, sir, it's still wet. At least, it is in that corner.'

Painted to order. Painting by numbers. Well, well. Louis was a bigger rogue than he'd thought.

'Get Higgins and the boy to take it down to the cellar. I'm going through to the study, and then I'll get ready for dinner.'

It was time for him to leave the pleasures of London and pay a visit to his old colleague Manfred Tauber again, in his stately mansion a few miles north of Oldminster. Manfred operated on a global scale but had never allowed the big picture to overshadow detail. He would know something about this appalling fake Virgin and Child, and why it should have been delivered to him here, in Chelsea.

Once in the study, he put through a call to Manfred Tauber.

* * *

Manfred Tauber looked at the invoice that Simon Bolt had handed to him.

'Ninety thousand pounds,' he said. 'The same sum as your son-in-law supposedly paid for his fake Giotto. Only, of course, it was you that he was defrauding all the time. He was never a victim — at least, not until someone decided that it was time for him to be taught a lesson. It wasn't you, was it?'

The two men had dealt in the money markets of the world for over forty years. Simon, harsh-voiced and domineering, knew how to bully and intimidate investors into parting with money, but had never been known to let his clients down. Manfred had the still watchfulness of a reptile. He never raised his voice — a voice renowned for its mellifluous tones — but his word was law in the various money markets where he traded. Colleagues and friends of a sort for over forty years, they had both earned the privilege of talking straight with each other.

'No, it wasn't me, but there were times when I felt tempted to help him out of this world! No, it's my theory that Louis went too far in his shady dealings, and some angry accomplice decided to silence him, maybe as a warning to others.'

They were sitting in the parlour of Grace Hall, where a low fire was burning in the Tudor grate. They had had lunch in the conservatory, a modern addition to the house overlooking a well-maintained formal garden.

'This was all your son-in-law's doing,' said Manfred Tauber. 'One-hundred-and-eighty-thousand pounds of your money in exchange for two worthless pictures. Money laundering, of course. I don't need to tell you that. And he took a million from you, which means the remaining money is lying in limbo somewhere. Leave it. It's pin money to you, Bolt.'

'Why did this painting turn up at my house in Chelsea?'

'Because somewhere along the line, someone confused the shipping and billing addresses, maybe because Louis Gillette was no longer around to keep a careful eye on things. It should have gone to Gillette's house in Oldminster. But then, I gather that he wasn't very good at anything he turned his hand to. You're well rid of him. Have you got a furnace in the basement of that house of yours? Burn the painting there, and move on. You and I are too old to spend time lamenting past swindles and their perpetrators.'

Williams had served them tall glasses of chilled Chablis, and with them had brought a box of perfumed, flat Bulgarian cigarettes. They drank and smoked in silence for a while, each occupied with his own thoughts.

Simon was thinking of a visit he had paid to Samuel Harker's gallery in an obscure lane near Westminster Cathedral not long after Louis's death. It had been at Harker's request. He had found a man in his forties, pale and quietly spoken, evidently in the first stages of spinal arthritis.

'Mr Bolt,' he'd said, 'I have here a painting that was bought by your late son-in-law. He paid me ninety thousand pounds for it, but it turned out to be a fake. I understand that he was in the habit of using your money to pay for such paintings. It would ease my conscience if you would accept ownership of it.'

'I will not,' Simon had replied. 'My daughter Lydia is Louis Gillette's next of kin — I'm not sure why you haven't approached her. I expect she will receive a refund from you for this mis-sold painting?'

Harker had appeared pained by the question. 'It's a very delicate matter,' he said, 'and at the moment is in the hands of my solicitors. You taking the painting would not affect all that, I assure you. You'll understand that I was only the intermediary in the transaction . . .'

And so he had left him, with nothing settled. He had left the painting, but had taken with him from that dim shop a fixed conviction that it was Samuel Harker who had murdered his son-in-law. He had had all the reptilian cunning of a professional assassin.

Manfred Tauber, too, was lost in thought. He was a thousand miles away, in Ukraine, listening to a cohort of dissidents plotting not an open revolt, but a gradual takeover of the economic institutions of the Ukrainian state. He had listened while they talked to him of underfunded industrial complexes, the need to strengthen the already warm relationship with China as a buffer against possible Russian aggression.

The leader of the dissidents, who had met with him secretly in a house on the outskirts of Kyiv, was Oleg Yanukovych, an undersecretary at the Ukrainian Interior Ministry, a man of clear ideas very much rooted in practicality.

It was one particular project of Yanukovych's that had caught Tauber's attention: a gas pipeline from Ukraine to Romania, Moldova, and so to the Baltic Sea. He had agreed to fund this, promising a sum that had sent Yanukovych reeling, on condition that, if ever he came to power, he would strengthen the country's already good relations with China. China, he said, could became a restraining influence on Russia, a country with a long memory.

And then he had flown to Beijing, where he had been received with that particular vigorous warmness that the People's Republic reserved for its foreign friends. He had thought then of his nervous guests at Grace Hall, frantically buying books from his celebrated collection, and he had smiled to himself.

'Don't worry, Bolt,' he said when he had aroused himself from his reverie. 'Put the past behind you. Don't let this painting nonsense get in the way of your business. The Treasury has just offloaded on to me a fresh pile of negotiable instruments that it doesn't want — bonds, long and short-term paper, and so on. If you want to dip a toe in the water, I'll bring you in at par. Are you sure you won't stay the night?'

'I must get back, my friend. Time waits for no man.'

'As you wish. But keep in touch, Bolt. We're living in precarious times.'

He accompanied his visitor to the door of the mansion.

'You think it was Samuel Harker who murdered your son-in-law, don't you? You may be right. But men like Harker are overreachers. One of these days, he'll go too far, and then he'll find himself in trouble.'

When Simon Bolt had gone, Manfred Tauber walked through the gardens of Grace Hall, ostensibly alone, but in fact watched by strategically placed guards who never let him out of their sight. It was understood in the household that these near-silent men were answerable only to him.

He walked through the kitchen garden, still maintained as such, and supplying fresh vegetables to the house, and pushed open a creaking gate which took him into a secluded private cemetery. He looked at the line of little graves containing the remains of long-dead pets: Fluffy, aged twelve. Selina, aged nine, Bertie, aged fourteen. There were others, some of them almost forgotten. Williams thought he was too sentimental about pets; maybe he was.

He came to a line of conventional headstones, their brief inscriptions giving merely a name, and the dates of birth and death. All had apparently died on the same day: 7 August 1985. Long-faded flowers, still covered by indestructible plastic, lay where he had placed them, long ago. He smiled to himself. Not one of those names was real.

The cemetery lay in a grove of trees, and deep in its centre was to be found a marble mausoleum, topped by the figure of an angel, eyes cast down, and holding a mourning wreath. The whole monument was stained with the droppings of sap exuded from the trees above it. Here lay his first wife, Magda, a woman as quietly fierce and single-minded as himself. When she had died of cancer, he had railed against Heaven, and even shook his fist at the sky . . . Useless. Here she lay till the last trumpet, and one day he would join her in this secret, artfully neglected spot.

'Williams thinks I'm growing soft,' he said aloud. 'You never knew Williams, *Liebchen*, but you would have approved of him. I let him see all — well, almost all — knowing that he would never let me down. I tested him, laid traps to see whether he would succumb to greed or corruption, but he proved himself to be incorrupt. I'm going now: I've work to do.'

Manfred Tauber left the cemetery, and made his way back to the house, watched at all times by his silent bodyguards.

* * *

Once back in London, it occurred to Simon Bolt to call upon the art dealer Samuel Harker again and retrieve the fake Giotto. Manfred had tacitly agreed with him that this crooked dealer, Samuel Harker, had murdered Louis to ensure his silence over the fraud that he'd perpetrated. There was no direct proof, but both heart and mind told Bolt that his son-in-law's murderer was likely to remain at large.

But he had plans for Samuel Harker. He had already identified the ground landlord of the man's premises near Victoria Street and had made him an offer that he couldn't refuse. His first step would be to evict the fellow, and then pursue him to abject ruin. Damn it! Louis was a rogue, but he had been his son-in-law, Lydia's husband.

He would start the whole process with Harker by agreeing to take Louis's fake Giotto, as though on Lydia's behalf.

It was an excuse to meet Harker face to face once again, to assess further what type of man he was, and where his vulnerabilities lay. He'd bring the Giotto home to Chelsea, and consign it to the furnace, where it could join the ashes of the fake Tintoretto.

Bolt's chauffeur brought his Mercedes to a halt at the entrance to the cobbled alley where Samuel Harker had his premises. It was just after four o'clock on a Saturday, but the place was very quiet. What a dismal, tawdry-looking place! He had to admit that Louis had made a conscious attempt to make his gallery in Oldminster appear stylish, even if he hadn't been much of an art dealer. Bolt mounted the three worn steps and pushed open the door.

There was no one around. Evidently, it was one of those shops where you had to shout for assistance unless you had an appointment. The walls were covered with framed oil paintings. At least the subjects were recognisable as people, not like the rubbish in Louis's place.

'Is there anyone there?' No answer.

Simon Bolt walked to the back of the shop and into what was evidently Harker's private office. He was sitting at a table, dead, his eyes wide open, his head thrown back, his arms flung out from his sides, the fingers twisted and rigid. On the table was a bottle of peach brandy, and a single wine glass. There was a strong smell of peaches in the air.

8. THE SAD FATE OF CHARLES DEACON

Saturday was takeaway night, and Glyn Edwards and his wife Sandra were enjoying a Chinese, which had been delivered by a lad from the Golden Gate in the High Street.

'That's where I interviewed Jack Prosser,' said Glyn, 'after he'd discovered the body of Louis Gillette in the Arcade. The Golden Gate.'

'It said in the *Gazette*,' said Sandra, 'that it might have been a suicide tricked out to look like a murder, though I can't see why anyone would want to do that.'

'No, love, it wasn't suicide. It was murder. His stomach was full of cyanide, but there was no sign of a glass or bottle in the room where he was found.'

Jack Prosser had been able to give the police a very different account of what had been in the room when he discovered the body of Louis Gillette, but Glyn could only tell Sandra so much. Prosser was still a 'person of interest'.

'I'll clear these things away, and we'll have some tea. *Midsomer Murders* is on at eight — mind, I don't want you laughing at the things they do. It's only a story . . .' She stopped and thought. 'Talking of ridiculous murders, how could you make someone swallow a glass of cyanide?'

'The obvious way is to disguise it as something else. Cyanide has a distinctive smell — think bitter almonds. We found a near-empty bottle of peach brandy laced with cyanide near to a dead vagrant behind the fish market, and we mapped out how it might have got there—'

'That was on Oldminster Live Radio,' said Sandra. 'I felt sorry for that poor man, reduced to living on the streets, and then being poisoned. So, you mapped out how it got there? The bottle in the alley, I mean.'

'Yes. I had to assume that the bottle of poisoned peach brandy had somehow or other been used to murder Louis Gillette. We know that a man carrying a holdall went into the Rembrandt Gallery, presumably with the bottle hidden in the holdall. After he'd committed the murder, he'd have put the bottle back, and left the gallery. He would have walked out of the Arcade, turned right into High Street, and then sharp right again into Potter's Lane. That would have brought him to the alley behind the fish market, where he would have got rid of the bottle in one of the commercial bins left out for next day's collection. Unfortunately, Sam Delaney — that was the vagrant's name — rifled through the bins, found the half-empty bottle, and drank the contents.'

Glyn had been talking to Sandra while she was making them two mugs of tea in the kitchen. She came in now, carrying a tray. He looked at her and thought of the terrible mental burdens she'd borne for so long, during all which time she had never neglected her appearance, always turned out smartly dressed and properly made up. *But she's got a lot of sympathy for people like Sam Delaney, though they're different on the surface,* he thought to himself. *She knows how it feels to be overwhelmed and lost.* Things were better now. Together they were painting the little box room upstairs for the reception of the baby girl that they were hoping to adopt.

'Where did the trail end?' she asked.

'Well, Inspector French and I thought we'd found it — we traced a bottle from the shop where it was bought to the man who bought it, a guy named Charles Deacon — and from him to Mr Manfred Tauber, the investment broker who lives out at Grace Hall. But the bottle of that particular peach brandy was still there in Tauber's wine cellar, so that proved to be a dead end. It's a very rare brandy, not the kind of thing you'd find in the average off-licence.'

They settled themselves in front of the television and drank their tea in silence for a while. Then Sandra spoke.

'I know how you could make a man drink a glass of cyanide,' she said. 'Say you're the killer, and this Louis Gillette had done you a great wrong — stolen money from you, or failed to pay a big debt. Something like that. Or he's been playing the field and you're the other woman he's just dumped.'

'Or his wronged wife?' Glyn suggested, playing along.

'Oh, not her. Lydia's such a nice woman — she's been a fundraiser for Oldminster Infirmary for years. Anyway, you decide that you're going to murder him.'

'So what do you do?'

'You pretend that you're going to forgive him, and ring him up to say that you want to meet him at his gallery, to make arrangements about his debt, or for one last — oh dear, that's not a very nice thing to say. We'll forget that.

'Anyway, I go along to Louis Gillette's gallery, and in that holdall you mentioned I have my bottle of poisoned brandy and two brandy glasses. Oh, did you find any brandy glasses?'

'No. There was nothing there, just the body. Go on, love.'

'Well, I go in there, and find Louis waiting for me. "Hello, old chap," or whatever people like that say, "all is forgiven. Let's drink to our new friendship." I open my hold-all, and take out the bottle of brandy and two glasses.

'Then I uncork the bottle, and pour out two glasses of brandy. Maybe I pretend to have a cold, and hold a hankie to my nose. I raise my glass. He raises his and knocks back the contents. Boom! He dies on the spot. Then I pour the contents of my glass back into the bottle, and . . . and . . .' She paused.

'Well, okay, there is a hole in my theory, isn't there? Why not leave the glass Louis has drunk from, and leave a fake note, to suggest suicide? Perhaps I won't give up the day job.' She sighed, and added, 'Did the bottle have a screw cap?'

Glyn Edwards looked at his wife with growing awe.

'Yes, it had a screw cap.' He wished he could tell her about the glass and the note that Jack Prosser had found and destroyed.

'So, anyway,' she went on, '*my* murderer — who is clearly cleverer than the actual murderer — slips away in the crowd at the Arcade, and makes his getaway. No one would notice him because it was the big sale day.'

'There were traces of cyanide in a small wash-hand basin in the gallery.'

'Oh, yes, well, I didn't pour my glass of cyanide back into the bottle. I poured it down the sink. A much simpler thing to do.'

Glyn Edwards thought, *She could well be right. Oh, don't be so jealous, of course she's right!* It was a brilliant solution to how the trick was done.

'Ingenious. The next vacancy we have for a detective, Sandra,' he joked, 'I'll put your name forward!'

She laughed. 'No fear. I don't fancy the hours.'

Work had once been a trigger for Sandra — she'd quit her job when she'd been very depressed, and for a long time she'd held on to a lot of guilt about his being the sole earner. He was glad she could laugh about it now and hadn't taken the joke the wrong way.

They began to watch *Midsomer Murders*, but Glyn couldn't pay attention. Sandra had always had a logical mind, and in this case had reasoned backwards from the deed to the killer's method. The killer had met his victim in the gallery, so therefore most probably by appointment. It had been essential not to alarm Louis Gillette, so he came as a man happy to forgive and forget. And then the wretched Jack Prosser had muddied the waters for everybody.

During the commercial break, Sandra offered another stunning observation — stunning, because it was so obvious, and yet he had never even given it any consideration.

'A man could buy two bottles of brandy,' she said, 'one to keep in his cellar, and the other to use as a weapon. Would you like a can of Budweiser?'

* * *

'It's certainly a valid theory,' said DI French. 'Look again into purchases of bottles of Lauretier Fils Grande Amber Peach Brandy. Check again with Mauleverer's Wine Merchants in Carlisle Street. Get them to check back in their books for a year. A murder of this kind could have been planned a good while ago. If you get no joy there, try the wine merchants in Chichester. I know it's Sunday, but we need to move things on.'

'What about online orders?'

'I get the feeling our killer won't want their name and address linked to this particular delivery. A cash purchase in person, possibly via a third party — that's our killer's style.'

'And that's Manfred Tauber's style, too. Where would our killer obtain his cyanide? You can't just buy it over the counter, or from a pharmacist.'

'If our killer is versed in Victorian garden lore, they'd know that you can make a distillation of cherry-laurel leaves — simple as that. Or it may have come from an industry where cyanide is used extensively, like mining. Or it may be that someone knows a laboratory where it can be synthesised to order. There are such places, as you know.' He thought for a while. 'It could be someone working in an industry, but someone willing to commit murder can be ingenious in such things. There was a case many years ago where a husband ordered cyanide to a company he wasn't connected to, and then intercepted the packages. The company got suspicious and contacted the police — it's how he was caught.'

'You think our killer might have done something similar?'

'I'm saying in this day and age, we'll be lucky to find the source. But let's keep looking for any reports of irregularities concerning cyanide records.'

* * *

Mauleverer's in Oldminster had not sold a bottle of Lauretier Fils Peach Brandy for over a year. Time to look further afield. It was at the third wine merchant's that he visited in the neighbouring city of Chichester that DS Edwards struck lucky. Thomas Mason & Co. had been trading in North Street since 1845 and were esteemed by connoisseurs of fine wines and spirits living in Sussex and beyond. Mr Mason, who looked more like a headmaster than a vintner, knew all about Lauretier Fils Grande Amber.

'We always keep a few bottles in the cellar here, sir,' he said. 'It's a point of honour not to run out of it! Cost? I offer it for thirty-five pounds. It's not wildly expensive, but it's considered a rare commodity in England. We import it directly from California.'

Glyn Edwards had shown Mr Mason his warrant card, and the wine merchant had been more than happy to expand on the subject of wines and spirits.

'A bottle of this brand of peach brandy was used to poison someone in Oldminster,' said Glyn. 'We were told — or we assumed — that it was very expensive.'

'No, Sergeant, but it's rare, what you might call an esoteric taste. I've brandies here costing hundreds of pounds.'

'And have you sold a bottle of Lauretier Fils Peach Brandy recently?'

'Let me see . . . This is the sales ledger, which I like to record in the old-fashioned way with pen and ink. I last sold a bottle on 14 August, which left me with four remaining in stock.'

'I don't suppose you can remember who you sold it to?'

'Well, as to that . . . I'm not a snob, Sergeant. Just because I deal in rare vintages doesn't mean that I look down on people who prefer a pint of bitter. But the man who bought that bottle of peach brandy wasn't the type of person we usually get in here. He was a shabby, defeated sort of man, quietly spoken, and — well, shifty, for want of a better word. He was clutching a twenty-pound note, and instead of asking me for the brandy, he presented me with a grubby piece of paper with the name written on it. He *looked* like a poisoner, now I come to think of it. Furtive. I read about that murder in the *Telegraph*. Perhaps he was one of these Russian spies, who come here to poison people they don't like.'

Perhaps, thought Glyn Edwards. Or perhaps it was Manfred Tauber's messenger boy, Charles Deacon.

* * *

'I've got an entry for him here, Glyn,' said Sergeant Lewis in Records, 'but it's nothing very special. Christmas week, 2014. Taken into custody for making a loud outcry in Town Hall Square, and for being drunk and incapable. Spent the night in Central lockup, appeared before the magistrate next morning, and let off with a caution because of his previous good behaviour. Nothing before or since. Hardly big time.'

'He's a sort of bagman for Manfred Tauber, the financier who lives the life of a country squire out at Grace Hall. He bought two bottles of peach brandy for him. One from Mauleverer's here in town, and the other from a wine merchant in Chichester. It was peach brandy laced with cyanide that was used to kill Louis Gillette, and which that poor vagrant drank when he found one of the bottles in the bins behind the fish market. I've interviewed Charles Deacon, who was a shifty individual with a fierce loyalty to Manfred Tauber, who paid off all his debts when he was in a really desperate plight.'

Pat Lewis was nearing retirement. He was a stout, slow-moving man who had sustained an injury to his arm in the course of duty, and had been permanently assigned to Records, a remote couple of rooms in the basement of Jubilee House, fitted out with racks to hold numerous cardboard box files.

'Manfred Tauber? I know of him. He's a good-hearted chap, a philanthropist, though I suppose you can afford to be nice when you're worth millions — or maybe billions.'

'Well, Pat, he sends this Charles Deacon out on forays to buy bottles of a rare peach brandy, the same make of brandy used to poison people with. I've nothing whatever against Tauber, but I don't like this connection of his with Deacon. Tauber's bought him, body and soul, and he'll have done that for a reason.'

'If this Deacon's as weak as you suggest, you could lean on him, Glyn, frighten him into talking. But I think you're barking up the wrong tree if you're suggesting that Manfred Tauber's up to no good. I know something about him, something that happened years ago, when I belonged to the Sacred Heart Social Club out at Mordale. Nineteen eighty-five, it was. A firm of contractors were clearing some scrub land on Tauber's estate when they uncovered a mass grave containing seven bodies. They had all been shot in the head. The bodies were all dressed in suits, and the upshot of it was that the police and some forensic experts said that they were all Poles, but they couldn't put names to them, or explain how they came to be buried on Tauber's land.'

'So what happened?'

'Mr Tauber hired some special investigators, who proved that the seven men had all been Polish exiles living here in Britain. They had all been active against the post-war Communist Polish Government, and it was almost certain that they had been lured to that remote spot on some pretence and shot by Communist agents. The Polish Government vigorously denied the accusations, and the matter was hushed up for the sake of international relations.'

'And where does the Sacred Heart Social Club fit in to all this?'

'Well, when Mr Tauber found out who they were, he had them put into expensive coffins, and arranged for a public Requiem Mass to be held in the church. Them being Poles, he assumed that they'd all been Catholics. And then he had them properly buried in the private cemetery attached to Grace Hall. That's the kind of man Tauber is, Glyn. Why should he want to poison an art dealer with doctored brandy?'

DS Edwards left Pat Lewis, and went back upstairs to DI French's office.

'There's been a development, Glyn,' said DI French. 'We've had a communication from Scotland Yard. Another art dealer's been poisoned with Lauretier Fils brandy laced with cyanide. This one's a London dealer, Samuel Harker, who delivered a fake Tintoretto to Simon Bolt's house in Chelsea. Bolt went to visit him on Saturday evening and found him dead in his shop.'

* * *

Charles Deacon's house in Moxton Hill looked defeated and depressed in the heavy rain that was falling when DS Edwards opened the gate and walked past the motorbike, still covered in its tarpaulin, now topped with a pool of rainwater.

'I played "good cop" when I called on him,' DI French had said. 'It's time for you to be "bad cop". He's a man with the jitters, who might break cover if you're stern enough. See if you can get Central to lend you PC Crane. She can stand at the gate and look official.' Well, it was too wet for young Anita Crane to stand at the gate, so he'd left her in the police car, which was advertisement enough for the street that the police had called at 6 Morrison Road.

Charles Deacon didn't seem keen to talk when he opened the door. 'Who did you say you were? Detective Sergeant Edwards? I've already spoken to a Detective Inspector French and told him everything I knew about the bottle of brandy.'

'Not everything, I think, Mr Deacon? You've bought that make of brandy elsewhere, haven't you? Like in

Chichester last August. You never told Mr French about that. Mr Tauber sends you on these errands, doesn't he? You're his errand boy. Did you also buy the hydrogen cyanide to mix with the contents?'

'What do you mean?' Deacon's voice rose to something like a shriek. 'Are you saying that I murdered that man? I can prove that I didn't. I was nowhere near the King's Arcade that night.'

'It's what we call being an accessory before the fact,' said Edwards. 'It makes you just as guilty as the person who actually committed the murder. You go away for at least twenty-five years. Why didn't you tell Inspector French about buying that bottle of brandy in Chichester?'

'It didn't seem relevant. Anyway, I've often gone into Chichester for things that Mr Tauber can't get here.'

'Do you have cyanide in your possession? I can get a search warrant, you know. At this stage I should warn you that you are within your rights to have a solicitor present during this interview, if you'd care to send for one.'

The man was white as a sheet and trembling, but so far had not incriminated himself in any way. Secretly Glyn Edwards thought that he was wasting his time. He'd make another wild, dramatic assertion, and then call it a day.

'With respect to the murdered Poles—'

Charles Deacon uttered a shriek and all but collapsed into a chair.

'I had nothing to do with it! Nothing! Those men were killed by Communist agents and secretly buried on Mr Tauber's land—'

'They were shot. Do you own a gun?'

'No. I'm a former bank clerk living on benefits. Mr Tauber was very generous in putting me back on my feet after a run of bad luck. I've never killed anyone. People like me don't go around killing people. We're victims, not perpetrators.'

'There may have been witnesses to those murders,' said Glyn. 'It's possible that statements will be made soon about the circumstances of those deaths. I'll leave you now, Mr Deacon.'

He rejoined PC Crane in the steamed-up car. She was watching the front window of the house through field glasses.

'He's phoning somebody now, sir,' said PC Crane. 'Warning someone, most likely. You don't think he's the killer, do you?'

'Not him, Anita. He's quite weak-looking, an alcoholic, according to DI French, and he's certainly not in good health. But he's tied up with something very shady, and if we wait long enough, he'll tell us what that "something" is.'

* * *

The man living in the half-ruined hunting lodge at Easton Peverell listened attentively to the voice at the other end of the line.

'I can't afford distractions of any kind. Not at this stage in the proceedings. So I want you to oblige me yet again. You'll find me very generous.'

'The London one was too clever by half,' said the man in the half-ruined hunting lodge. 'Not my style at all, though it seems to have come off very well. Are you sure you can't take a different course of action? I'm rather conservative about this kind of thing. If there's to be a series, I like them to be judiciously spaced out.'

'I'm quite sure. There are times when I can be very accommodating, but this is not one of them, I'm afraid. There's no choice but murder. See to it, will you?'

* * *

Extract from the *Oldminster Gazette*, late edition. Wednesday, 3 October 2018:

Moxton Hill Man Found Drowned
 Charles Deacon, 57, of 6 Morrison Road, Moxton Hill, was found drowned at Bishop's Park Ponds early this morning, by a couple walking their dog. James Peake, a park

ranger, told the Gazette that the body had been floating face downward in the Lesser Pond, where there are rowing boats, and it was he who had rowed out and recovered the body.

A neighbour of Charles Deacon, who wished to remain anonymous, told our reporter: 'Mr Deacon had been in very low spirits recently, having been unemployed for some time. Mrs Deacon has gone to stay with her mother until the police release her husband's body for burial.'

The Gazette contacted Oldshire Police headquarters at Jubilee House, but they refused to comment.

* * *

'I did what I could for Charles Deacon, Williams,' said Manfred Tauber. 'I was more than happy to use him to run errands and so forth. But there . . . These things don't always work out as you'd hope.'

'Had you known him long, sir?'

'I knew him for years. Like me, he was a local man, and at one time he worked in the Oldminster branch of my little retail banking group that I sold to NatWest. Well, not exactly sold: I allowed them to acquire it, put it that way. He was a counter clerk, but not a very successful one. NatWest felt that they had to let him go.'

'I only came across him recently.'

'Yes, his useful days were largely over before you came to work for me. He proved himself to be quite handy carrying out little jobs for me on the estate, and I'd give him the occasional tenner. Years ago, he helped me with that cemetery business. I gave him a thousand pounds for his help over that affair, but he never knew how to build on income, however small.'

'You paid off all his debts not long ago.'

'Yes, and O'Toole thought I was going soft. Maybe you did too! But I was shaping some kind of a future for Charles Deacon. Well, there it is. He's gone. In the long term, he proved to be one of my very rare bad investments.'

* * *

'He wasn't well at all,' said Dr Raymond Dunwoody. 'There was what we call a "shadow" on his left lung, and his liver was badly compromised.'

'And he drowned?' asked DI French.

'No, he didn't. There was no water in his lungs. As soon as I opened his stomach with the scalpel I smelt the bitter almonds—'

'What?' DI French jumped up from his desk. 'You don't mean—'

'Yes, it was murder, Paul. There were signs of what I'd better call mild manual strangulation on the neck. And SOCO told me that the back of his jacket held traces of grass and soil. I'll tell you what I think happened — this won't be in my official report, because it's merely supposition.

'Charles Deacon was thrown to the ground by a strong individual who held him helpless by placing a knee on his chest. He then constricted his throat long enough to make him open his mouth, and then he poured prussic acid down his throat.'

'So we've three murders by cyanide — Louis Gillette, this man Harker in London, and now Charles Deacon. That poor vagrant was what they call collateral damage.'

'Precisely. But I think there's more to it than that. Why dump the body in a pond where it's easy to find? Whoever this killer is, he's mocking us, Paul. He's having a laugh at our expense, because he knew that we would conduct a post-mortem and find the cyanide. He thinks he's cleverer than the police; perhaps he is. We still don't know why these murders were committed, but this new element — taunting the police — makes me wonder whether our killer has illusions of grandeur, whether, in fact, he's becoming unhinged.'

* * *

Lance Middleton, QC, was back home in his chambers in Lincoln's Inn. He still ached from the assault in Waterloo but had already begun his investigation in pursuit of Simon

Bolt's lost million pounds. He sat now at his round dining table, savouring a plate of pan-fried turbot fillets with mushrooms, ginger and soy broth, brought directly to him from the kitchens of a nearby French restaurant with whom he had a long-standing arrangement. It was to be followed by a confection of fresh berries steeped in brandy. To help this meal down he had opened a bottle of chilled Hock.

He had heard from the police that morning that they had caught the tattooed thug, a muscle-for-hire type by the name of Pete Taylor, who was naming no names, perhaps because he didn't know the true identity of the person who had hired him. Lance hoped they threw the book at him.

Samuel Harker, the money launderer, had been put to silence, but in the context of these cyanide killings, he was small fry. There were bigger fish to catch, and tomorrow he would embark on his quest. Meanwhile, he would give his undivided attention to the turbot fillets.

9. LYDIA MEETS AN OLD FRIEND

Lydia Gillette stood in front of the fireplace in the drawing room of the house in Gladstone Road, observing herself in the mirror. She had just returned from London, where she had collected from a prominent women's tailor in Savile Row a costume suit of deepest black, which she would wear during the day with a double string of pearls.

People would think that she was living in the nineteenth century — who in these enlightened times had themselves fitted out with 'widow's weeds'? But she had to do something to show that she was genuinely mourning the husband whom she had betrayed.

She was still handsome and attractive, but her days now belonged to Louis. Had he really planned to leave her? Perhaps he would have sent for her when he was ready. That's what Claudia Hurst had suggested, and Felicity Campbell had agreed with her. But perhaps they had done so merely to help assuage her sadness.

Jack Prosser had written to her, begging her forgiveness, and hinting that they should get together again soon. She had burnt his letter and left it unanswered. Their illicit romance was over, the memories of their more innocent days together as teenagers now finished and forgotten. He had violated Louis's death scene out of some kind of warped sense of obligation to her. What kind of man did a thing like that? Poor Louis — would his killer ever be caught now that the evidence had been destroyed? Well, Jack Prosser could go his own way. She had no desire to see him ever again.

Daddy was right. Despite her protests that she belonged to Oldminster, she would be safer with him in London, far away from the city where her mother and her husband had been doomed to die. She would sell this house, and perhaps rent a flat in Mayfair, and start a new life there. Felicity Campbell had embraced the idea of 'good works' as the badge of her widowhood. Perhaps she would do the same.

A ring at the doorbell roused her from her reverie. Who could this be, calling mid-morning? When she opened the front door, she found herself looking at a handsome, middle-aged man wearing a tailored overcoat. His hair was silvered at the temples, but his neatly trimmed moustache was still black.

'Lydia,' said the caller, 'may I come in?' He treated her to a quizzical smile. 'You've forgotten me, haven't you? I'm Rupert Danecourt.'

'Oh! Rupert! Come in! It must be thirty years or more since I saw you last.'

She had not seen Rupert Danecourt since the late 1980s. He had been one of Louis's friends, when Louis had begun his successful courtship, and Jack Prosser had gone off, raging and tearful when she had announced her engagement to Louis. What happy times they had been! While she'd reserved a special place for Jack in her heart, she had enjoyed being a young wife with a charming husband who was going to make his way in the art world, and the friends they had made, entertaining in each other's homes, and going out together to parties, concerts, picnics . . .

Rupert, too, had married young. He and his wife, Julie, a lively, fine-featured woman, had both worked in a publisher's office in Chichester. Rupert had been a stunningly handsome young man, and he had lost none of his good looks in early middle age.

'Let me take your coat, Rupert,' said Lydia. 'Sit here, by the fire. I'll make us some coffee.'

'I read about Louis in the *Uckfield News*,' said Rupert. 'I was going to write but thought a visit would be better. You look — you look very nice, Lydia. But then, you always did.'

She made them coffee and sat opposite him by the fire.

'Did you stay in publishing?' she asked. 'I'm sorry we lost contact. All those friends we had — I don't hear from any of them, now.'

'Yes, I stayed in publishing. Have you heard of the Marlborough House Press? Well, that's me. And I have other businesses connected with the book trade — distributing, art publishing. Did you ever take up a profession?'

'No . . . I was content to be Louis's wife and support. I expect you know that he ran the Rembrandt Gallery in the King's Arcade.'

'Yes, of course I do. Julie and I used to come to those sherry parties that you held there on exhibition days. Don't you remember? Is he — is he buried here in Oldminster? I'd very much like to visit his grave, leave some flowers, that sort of thing. We were quite good friends, you know.'

'Louis's in the churchyard, just a step away from here. What about you? Did you . . .'

'After Julie died, I threw myself into my work. Like you, we had no children.'

She watched him as he sipped his coffee. There seemed nothing defeated about him. He looked content with his lot, steady, dependable. A successful man, unspoilt by time. Would he ask about Jack Prosser? She hoped not.

'I'm thinking of moving away. Daddy's in London; I might take a flat there to be near him,' she said. 'There's nothing here for me now, really.' She saw Rupert stir uneasily and wondered why.

'That gallery,' he said. 'What do you propose to do with it? I suppose the premises are leased?'

'They are, but Louis owed three months' rent, which I've just now paid off. Louis had taken out a very decent life insurance, which more than covered that debt.'

Why on earth was she talking of private matters like this to a man she'd not seen for thirty years? She suddenly remembered something that Chloe had told her about a friend of hers, Caleb Brewster. This man, who had been present at the gallery reception on 11 September, had told her that Louis should abandon selling artworks of dubious value, and start up a proper workshop and gallery space, selling local crafts and providing a space for art classes. There was nothing like that in Oldminster. Was there, perhaps, something that she could do about that? No, best get rid of the place where her husband had been so vilely murdered.

'You know, Lydia,' Rupert said, 'I've no right to walk in off the street like this and ask you impertinent questions. But when you said that you'd join your father in London, it seemed to me that you were contemplating running away— No, hear me out, and if you don't like what I say, then I'll take my leave.

'You've lived here since you were ten years old — yes, I remember all that. I remember your mother, and how terrible it was when she died when you'd just turned twenty. Your father was in London, but you married Louis, and put down more roots here. Oldminster is where you belong, not London. So why are you running away?'

'I was never meant to be alone,' she said. 'It's wonderful to have good friends, and I have many here, but that's not the same as having a husband, or a partner. All I can do now is sit around in this big draughty house, with occasional sorties into town, or to meetings of the Cathedral Ladies' Guild.'

Rupert Danecourt made no reply. He sat quite still, just looking at her. What more did he expect her to say? He was right, of course. And the real reason she wanted to get away from Oldminster was because Jack Prosser was still there. She dreaded meeting him by chance in town, dreaded the thought that he might turn up in Gladstone Road one day, asking her to forgive him.

Because she knew that, once face to face with him, she would almost certainly yield to him. That would be a double betrayal of her dead husband. The idea of that confrontation filled her with terror.

'So that gallery,' said Rupert, mercifully changing the subject, 'what are you going to do with it? If you did decide to stay here, in Oldminster, you could do all kinds of interesting things with the premises.'

'Somebody told a friend of mine that Louis should have turned it into an artists' collective space — you know the sort of thing, a workshop, classes, local art. But — well, poor Louis was murdered in that shop.'

Even as she spoke, she glimpsed the lure of independence. Daddy would always be there to support her, but it would boost both her confidence and her self-respect if she could earn her own living.

She saw Rupert glance at his watch, and she put out a silent plea: *Don't go!*

'It's nearly twelve,' she said. 'Won't you stay to lunch? I can do some sandwiches, and I've plenty of fresh fruit.'

'I'd love that, Lydia,' said Rupert Danecourt. 'An artists' collective, you say? How many rooms are there in the gallery? I can't quite remember.'

'Three — quite big rooms. And there's a little washroom, and a kind of storeroom — more a large cupboard, really.'

'Hm . . . I've not been to Oldminster for some years, but I do remember that the Arcade was full of exclusive shops. You might think of stocking some high-quality prints alongside the local stuff, both for framing, and for sale as greetings cards. Pre-Raphaelite stuff always goes down well.'

'But Rupert, there is a bookshop in the Arcade already and they sell cards—'

'You can work with your neighbours to make sure you're not stepping on anyone's toes. And if the bookshop doesn't already sell them, you might sell some attractive and appealing art books, too, which might draw people in from the expensive stores and fund some of the other things you're thinking of. I can give you contacts for all those things. Three rooms? You could have a few small tables and serve coffee and cakes. People would be tempted by that. If that mini café became popular, you could put it out to franchise. I could help you there, too.

'Oh, and picture framing,' Rupert continued. 'And bespoke stationery, and so on. You could draw in a little coterie of experts in things like that. Mutual dependence to everybody's advantage . . .'

Lydia listened, fascinated. Rupert was virtually talking to himself, but he was creating a vivid picture of what could be a major part of her coming to terms with Louis's death. She could see herself working in a refurbished gallery — she would keep the name that Louis had given it.

'You'd need to let a firm of shopfitters loose on it,' said Rupert. 'They would erase all traces of — of what happened there, but it would still be Louis's gallery, if you see what I mean. He would still be there, in spirit. Well, not exactly that, but you know what I mean. Otherwise, the whole place will be stripped bare to its basic fittings, with horrible red-and-white "For Lease" signs stuck on the windows. Oh, dear me, Lydia, have I gone too far? I only called here to convey my condolences!'

'I'll make those sandwiches,' said Lydia. She felt exhilaration at the prospect that Rupert had opened up. No more sitting by herself in her empty house. No more looking to Daddy to keep her solvent. She would have to cope with the shadow of Jack Prosser as best she could, but he must not be allowed to drive her out of her own home. As she went into the kitchen, she could see the shop that Rupert Danecourt had created in her mind's eye. It was more vivid to her than the present reality of her bland, oatmeal house.

After lunch, they walked down Gladstone Road to All Saints church, and she took him to the secluded spot where Louis Gillette lay. It was a warm October day, with a pale sun shining. In a year's time she would have a black granite stone erected, with an inscription in incised gold letters. In her mind's eye she could see some parts of what would be written there: *Beloved Husband of Lydia*, and the text from Lamentations that Canon Murchison had told her was often put on the gravestone of a murder victim: *O LORD thou hast seen my wrong: judge thou my cause.*

Lydia began to cry, and Rupert put a hesitant hand on her arm. There was no guilt being with this man, an old friend of both of them, standing so near to Louis where he lay. She suddenly felt that a voice was urging her to draw closer to Rupert, an urgent, familiar voice, but one that could not be actually heard. It was more a kind of impulse, perhaps a rationalising of her own instant attraction to Rupert, but Lydia knew that it was more than that.

'I don't know whether there was any trouble between you two,' said Rupert, 'but you can be quite certain that Louis has forgiven you, as I'm sure you've forgiven him.' He paused. 'I don't know what made me say that. It's time for me to get on the road. As I told you at lunch, I live in Uckfield, but I'd like to visit Oldminster more often in future.'

'That would be nice,' said Lydia. 'If I'm to do as you suggest, I would need a loan. Perhaps Daddy—'

'Might I offer some advice? You seemed pleased at the thought of striking out on your own. Family and money don't always mix, especially if the person with the money likes to be in control. If I were in your position, I would take out a commercial loan, and repay it from your profits. I can put you in touch with some very good people for transactions of that kind. That way, it will be your own venture from the start.'

They stood in silence for a while, looking down at the wreaths lying on Louis's grave.

'I didn't mean to suggest anything against your father,' he said, more gently. 'Have I overstepped the mark?'

She shook her head. 'You've given me a lot to think about. I'm glad you came, Rupert.'

They made their way out of the churchyard arm in arm.

* * *

121

Lance Middleton QC sat in the back bar of the King William Arms, a crowded pub in an obscure alley off St Swithin's Lane in London's East End. The lane was renowned for housing the London headquarters of the Rothschild Bank, but the alley was frequented by a much more obscure class of people, at least, with respect to the clientele of the King William Arms. The men in the bar — they were all men — drank deep, and talked quietly. They were mostly dressed in black. They were all elderly, a congregation of white heads.

Lance Middleton was not alone at one of the little round tables — one of the dark-suited men had peeled away from the fraternity when he had entered in order to sit with him. His companion was in his seventies, or thereabouts.

'You know me, Mr Heathersage,' said Lance. 'I'm not a mischief maker, and I don't break confidences. But if anyone can help me on my way in this business, it'll be you. Is that whisky to your liking?'

'It is, Mr Middleton. Very kind of you to get it for me. What seems to be the problem?'

'How could a failing art gallery owner in a provincial city swindle Simon Bolt out of a million pounds? Or more to the point, how could he pull the wool over the eyes of Bolt's accountant, a man called Nathan Buckley.'

Mr Heathersage smiled, revealing a mouthful of irregular and stained teeth.

'You look rather the worse for wear, Mr Middleton,' he said. 'Have you been in a fight? Somehow, I don't associate you with fisticuffs. The trouble with Nathan Buckley is that he's relaxed his vigilance. He's so accustomed to dealing with Simon Bolt's millions that he farmed out some of Bolt's accounts to other accountants, who acted in his name — Buckley's, I mean. Farming out can be a perilous practice.'

'Can you elaborate on that? You know so many things, Mr Heathersage.'

'I don't always remember things, you know, Mr Middleton. I'm getting old, and my memory's not what it was.'

Lance Middleton felt in his pocket and brought out a fifty-pound note, which he placed on the table, near to his companion's whisky glass.

'But in the matter of your gallery owner, I can recall quite clearly the train of events. That man — Louis Gillette — had been playing with fire for years, borrowing where he could, then borrowing to pay the lenders. Perhaps it was inevitable that he fell in with Samuel Harker, another art dealer. I expect you know all about Samuel Harker?'

'I do.'

'Well, Harker found Gillette a willing pupil in the school of villainy. It was Harker who found a crooked accountant for the farming out of some of Bolt's accounts. I know who that man was, but I'll not reveal his name. Harker ran one of the most profitable money-laundering businesses in Europe, based on the idea of clients paying for so-called works of art. Well, you know all about that, I expect. Harker's crooked accountant syphoned off a million pounds from Bolt's accounts, and Harker took a commission of one-hundred-and-eighty-thousand, which he then shared with the crooked accountant. That's how it was done. Then it was Harker's turn to go too far, and somebody topped him for it. Do you see that ginger-haired man standing at the bar? Mention my name to him, and he might have something interesting to tell you. I must be off. Very nice to have seen you again, Mr Middleton.'

Mr Heathersage swept up the fifty-pound note, and left the crowded bar.

Lance Middleton recalled the case of Regina v. Heathersage, which had been tried at the Old Bailey five years previously. 'My Lord, my client had no idea that he had been part of a wicked fraudulent transaction. His fault is that he is too innocent and too trusting.' It had been a prolonged battle with the prosecuting counsel, but he had won the case, and Heathersage had gone free. Neither the acquitted man nor his counsel ever said a word about the case, but Lance Middleton always had an uneasy feeling that his client had, in fact, been guilty.

The red-headed man at the bar had clearly been expecting him.

'The man you're looking for is called Edmund Salis,' he said. 'He's an accountant with offices in Crutched Friars. You don't know me, Mr Middleton, so you can't say who told you about Salis. But it certainly wasn't Bill Heathersage.'

When Lance Middleton got back to his chambers in Lincoln's Inn, he put through a call to Noel Greenspan in Oldminster.

'Noel, is that you? Can you come up to London this coming Monday? We've a very good chance of getting Simon Bolt's million pounds back . . . Yes, tell Chloe, by all means, but I think it had better be you who comes this time, if she agrees. Technically we're acting for Lydia Gillette, but it was Simon Bolt's money that her husband stole. Can you bring a "heavy" with you? Just in case anybody wants to chuck me down the stairs again. Do you know any "heavies"? You do? Good. See you this coming Monday, then.'

* * *

They found Edmund Salis in his office at the Fenchurch Street end of Crutched Friars. His premises were above a jeweller's shop, and accessed by means of a steep flight of carpeted stairs. It was a neat, tidy place, and Mr Edmund Salis looked like a neat, tidy man. He rose up from his desk in alarm when Noel Greenspan and Lance Middleton entered, accompanied by an enormous bruiser of a man who stood in front of the door when it had been closed. The man's flabby face seemed to be devoid of all expression.

'Who are you? What do you want?' Mr Salis's voice was high and strident. He was a small, slim man, somewhat under average height, clean-shaven, and with thinning grey hair.

'My name is Noel Greenspan. I am a private detective retained by the Bolt family of Oldminster. This gentleman is Lance Middleton, QC, also acting in the family's interest. The man by the door is my associate, Mr Gogg.'

'What do you want?' Edmund Salis repeated.

'Really, you know very well what we want,' said Noel. 'We want Mr Bolt's money back. A million pounds, to be exact. We know that you're a thief and a robber, you see, and very soon our own accountant will be taking your books apart to uncover how you deceived Nathan Buckley. It took him months to realise that an enormous sum of money had gone missing from his books.'

'This is outrageous! I'm going out now, to fetch the police!'

'Do so by all means, that is, if you can get past Mr Gogg.'

As the quaking accountant neared the door, Mr Gogg lunged forward. Salis whimpered with fright and grabbed for his phone.

'As to the police,' said Noel Greenspan, and at his words Salis froze, 'we have friends in high places — at a word from me you will be arrested. Give us back the million pounds. We'll get it out of you one way or another.'

Edmund Salis had gone deathly pale. He sat down quietly at his desk, setting the phone down before him. It was Lance's turn to speak.

'Of course,' he said, 'it's just possible that you made a careless mistake, due to handling accounts with which you were unfamiliar. Perhaps you misunderstood instructions, and arranged certain bank transfers without thinking what you were doing.'

The drowning man clutched at the straw.

'Yes, yes, that's what must have happened. Over-confidence on my part—'

'In which case,' said Lance, 'we would be happy if you would rectify that error, now, and give us the money back. No tricks, mind. These are dangerous times. Look what happened to your friend Samuel Harker.'

'Harker? Yes, very sad. All this has been a misunderstanding. I'll write you a cheque—'

'No cheques, please, Mr Salis,' said Noel Greenspan. 'Cash, negotiable bonds, or a mixture of both. And that will be the end of the matter.' He tried not to blush at the lie — he had already reported the whole thing to the police, who were on their way. He had hoped to record a fuller admission of guilt, but even the conversation as it stood would show that Salis didn't deny removing the money from Simon Bolt's account.

Edmund Salis opened a safe, withdrew a folder containing a sheaf of Treasury bonds. To this the trembling man added several wads of one-hundred pound notes.

'What about Buckley?' he asked. 'You say he knows about my defalcations?'

'He does, but we have persuaded him to hold his tongue,' lied Lance smoothly. 'He will merely dispense with your services.'

The police raided Salis's offices not long after. By late afternoon on the following day, the bonds had been cashed, and the whole sum of one million pounds had been deposited in Simon Bolt's bank.

When his daughter Lydia told him what her friend Noel Greenspan and her associates had done, he was more than fulsome in his praise. He invited Lance Middleton to his house in Chelsea, where he entertained him to a sumptuous dinner prepared by his Swiss chef. It was a meal that the gourmet QC long remembered.

Greenspan and McArthur, private detectives, received a generous pay out for their services.

* * *

Extract from the late edition of the *London Evening Standard*, 11 October 2018.

> *Body found. — The body of Edmund Salis, 54, accountant, of Marigold Street, Maida Vale, was found by a visitor to his house this morning. Salis was found sitting at a table in his dining room. A wineglass and a medicine bottle standing on the table were later found to contain cyanide. He was a widower, with no children. An inquest will be opened tomorrow.*

10. THE GANG OF SEVEN

'Lance Middleton did a fantastic job in London,' said DS Edwards. 'He actually tracked down the man who'd relieved Simon Bolt of his million pounds and made him give it back.'

'I grant you he was very clever to track him down, or perhaps I should say well connected,' said DI French, 'but he also muddied the waters for the rest of us: he's not restrained by the requirements of police procedure, and that means that many more crooked tax-dodgers who Salis worked with will likely never be brought to justice. That swindling accountant should have been prosecuted, but Middleton's actions gave him time to destroy the evidence of further crimes. What would it have harmed Simon Bolt to wait for his money a little longer while the prosecutor assembled a case?'

'But the police raided Salis shortly after Lance and Noel were there — he wouldn't have had time, sir.'

French tutted and harrumphed as he studied the report from his counterpart at the Metropolitan Police. 'Perhaps that's so, Glyn. Middleton told me Edmund Salis actually had a million pounds in his safe. People like Salis have access to vast sums of money. They seem like fortunes to the likes of you and me, but to Salis and others like him it's just chicken feed. And now he's dead, too, another cyanide victim. Gillette, Harker, Deacon, Salis. It's becoming an epidemic.'

'That's the Met's business, sir,' said Glyn. 'Unless you want to tie our investigations to theirs?'

'No, let's not complicate matters. I don't like Middleton and his like freelancing and putting themselves in danger. Noel Greenspan's different: he's a licensed private detective — he should have known better than to play the enforcer.'

'I suppose they let their emotions get the better of them, after the attacks on Lance and Chloe.'

'Pure vigilantism. It won't do, Glyn. I shall have to have a word with Noel. But where have we got to, so far? Nowhere. Superintendent Philpot's talking about bringing in Scotland Yard.'

Neither man commented on this statement. They let the threat of Scotland Yard hang in the air.

'This cyanide — it must all be one person, Glyn. The modus operandi is too similar. It all started here, in Oldminster, with Louis Gillette, and that unfortunate tramp. And then it moved to London, to that man Harker, and now to Edmund Salis. And Charles Deacon, of course.'

'What about Simon Bolt, sir? He'd been swindled by Louis Gillette. Could he have been ruthless enough to murder him?'

'You're not thinking straight this morning, Sergeant. We're not dealing with the Godfather here. Bolt's a bit of a bully, but he's straight as a die. Can you imagine him travelling down from London to Oldminster with a holdall full of cyanide? He's not exactly inconspicuous.'

'All the same, sir—'

'Oh, very well — we'd better check he has an alibi for the first murder, at least. Though I suppose a man of Bolt's wealth might hire a hit man — an alibi wouldn't help us there.'

'Then there's the Lauretier Fils Grande Amber Peach Brandy.'

'Yes, and don't forget what your Sandra said: a man can buy two bottles of brandy if he so wishes. Words to that effect, anyway. Go out to Grace Hall again, Glyn, and have a good nose around. I'll admit that I didn't probe deeply enough last time — I only spoke to the house manager, John Williams, and didn't trouble the owner of the house. Back then I was only interested in a bottle of peach brandy, and when I found it was there I discounted the Taubers from my list of suspects. But now I'm thinking of alibis. You suggested that Simon Bolt could have come down here to do away with his son-in-law. Well, I'm sure that he could produce an impeccable alibi if we were cheeky enough to ask him. But what about Manfred Tauber? Where was he on the day of Gillette's murder?'

'But what,' asked Glyn, trying to contain his rising confusion, 'what has Manfred Tauber to do with Louis Gillette?'

'Perhaps you should ask him. In the nicest possible way, of course.'

* * *

Glyn Edwards hadn't been to Grace Hall before, and he was somewhat taken aback at the grand driveway and picturesque mansion. The door was answered by a harassed-looking maid who showed him to 'the parlour' — a vast room with a stunning view of the grounds that had something of the look of a flower shop about it, thanks to a bunch of roses and tulips upended on the floor. A smartly dressed man was picking up broken ceramic from the floor while a pale young maid looked on in dismay.

'Oh, Martha,' he said as he saw the maid who had shown in Glyn, 'would you tidy this up? Poor Greta's not having the best of mornings. And you must be DS Edwards?' He went on without hesitation as he stepped away from the mess and the two women hurried to clean away the spillage. 'Please excuse me for not answering the door myself — I'm in the midst of preparations for a party next week — just a thank-you dinner for Mr Tauber's clients. I must admit I was curious when you phoned. This isn't about that bottle of peach brandy again, is it?'

'I have to admit, Mr Williams,' said DS Glyn Edwards, 'that we are making very slow progress in the case of Louis Gillette's murder. That's why we're now renewing our process of eliminating people from our investigation by establishing alibis.'

'Alibis, you say? What date were you thinking of?'

'The night of the fourteenth of September. But I don't want an alibi from you, Mr Williams. I need to ask Mr Tauber himself.'

'Ask what of Mr Tauber?'

Manfred Tauber had come into the parlour in the company of his wife, Corinne. Glyn Edwards thought, *What a beautiful woman, and what wonderful clothes she's wearing. She must be in her thirties, while he's what? Seventy-five?*

'This is Detective Sergeant Edwards, sir, from the Oldshire Police.'

'How do you do, Sergeant? And what can I do for you?'

'I'm conducting enquiries, sir, concerning the murder of Louis Gillette — we're eliminating any remotely connected parties. I'd like you to tell me where you were on the night of Friday the fourteenth of September.'

He waited for the storm, but none came.

'The fourteenth? Was that the day on which Louis Gillette was murdered? Well, let me see. I was here all that evening, wasn't I, Corinne?'

'What? Oh, probably — wasn't I away that evening? Williams will tell you.'

'Yes, Sergeant, it was one of those days when Mr Tauber had some precious free time to himself. Ask any of the staff. They'll confirm he was here.'

'Thank you, sir.' He remembered Tauber's connection to Charles Deacon, and added quickly, 'And can I also ask where you were on the afternoon and evening of Tuesday the second of October, and the early hours of Wednesday the third of October?'

Tauber looked thoughtful. 'Much the same, I expect. Williams?'

Williams was already looking at a calendar on his phone. 'I believe that was when you were on your European jaunt, sir.'

'Out of the country,' Glyn said woodenly, writing in his notebook.

Well, well, thought Glyn. *I wonder if that's true. You've all been a bit too glib for your own good.*

'Well, thank you, Mr and Mrs Tauber,' he said. 'I'm relieved that you didn't take offence at my request. These are purely routine procedures, but they have to be carried out. I hope you enjoy your party next week.'

'Thank you, Sergeant. Well, it's time for Mrs Tauber and me to go out to a fundraising affair here at the village hall. The best of luck with your investigations.'

'Do you want to examine the bottle of peach brandy again?' asked Williams, as he accompanied DS Edwards to the door. His tone was neutral, but Glyn could sense that he was inwardly hugging himself with glee.

'No, thank you, Mr Williams. You heard that Mr Tauber's errand boy Charles Deacon was murdered? It looked like a drowning, but it was in fact murder by cyanide. I expect Mr Tauber was very upset.'

'He was. He doesn't like to talk about it. Deacon worked for him once, and he was very kind to him when he fell on hard times. Very kind indeed.'

They were all inscrutable, and too smooth by half.

Once free of Williams, DS Edwards wandered through the extensive grounds of the old mansion. He was remembering what Pat Lewis in Records had told him about the Polish exiles buried in Tauber's private cemetery. They could have nothing to do with the present case, but nevertheless they were of interest. Why were they buried here, where they had been found, rather than in regular cemeteries? Where were their loved ones?

He found the secluded spot beyond the kitchen garden, pushed open the gate and went in.

A strange, weird place. Here were some pets' graves. And here were the graves of the Polish men, seven identical headstones all bearing Polish names, and the same date of death, 7 August 1985, well over thirty years ago. He took out his notebook, and copied the names, stumbling over the many c's, z's and w's that seemed to characterise the Polish language. Would it be a waste of police time to re-examine the story of these long-dead men? Perhaps. But there was a certain place in Oldminster where he would almost certainly get some honest answers to his questions.

* * *

The Polish Centre occupied two shops in Archway Road, a busy thoroughfare to the south of the train station. As on his previous visit in connection with another case, DS Edwards found the place to be a hive of activity. People were filling out forms of various kinds, assisted by an elderly man in a baggy suit. A couple of men were playing pool, while others were watching Sky Sports in a back room. The elderly man looked up and smiled in recognition.

'Detective Sergeant Edwards! We meet again! What can I do for you? Come upstairs, and we'll have a cup of tea.' He spoke perfect English, without a trace of an accent.

'Nice to see you again, Mr Milczarek. I want you to help me with a history project.'

They went upstairs to a room overlooking the street, a kind of office and reference library with a sink and draining board by the window. The manager of the Polish Centre brewed them two mugs of tea and listened while Glyn Edwards told him of his visit to the private cemetery at Grace Hall.

When he had finished, Glyn handed him his notebook, so that he could read the names that he had copied from the headstones. Milczarek looked at the names for what seemed like minutes. His usually friendly, open countenance was transfigured by a sudden austere reserve.

'Some things, my friend,' he said, 'things that happened in the past, are best left buried. Because things long-buried and then dug up can spring to life again and bite you.

Manfred Tauber knows all about these men, and so does Her Majesty's Government. Leave the Gang of Seven in the past.'

'The Gang of Seven? So they were something more than Polish exiles?'

'These names,' said Mr Milczarek, 'Henryk Sienkiewicz, Boleslaw Prus, Kazimierz Zalewski — they're all Polish novelists of the nineteenth century. Sienkiewicz was the author of *Quo Vadis*, and a Nobel prize winner. He's certainly not buried in the grounds of Grace Hall.' He tapped the page with a finger. 'And these others are Polish artists and composers.'

He handed the notebook back to Glyn, and sat in silence, looking at him. Glyn thought, *At last!* Something decidedly fishy connected with Manfred Tauber. Seven men, supposedly Polish exiles, buried in obscure graves under assumed names. And this decent, normally friendly man knew something about them — knew who they were, probably. But was it too dangerous a secret to share with others?

'Manfred Tauber is well respected in Oldshire,' said Milczarek at last. 'He supports many charities, and I will tell you at once that during the war his German relatives did all they could to alleviate the wretched lot of the Poles. One of them was decorated by the West German Government for his resistance to Hitler's terror.'

'But you said something about the Gang of Seven? Who were they?' Glyn persisted.

'If you want details, you can ask Interpol. I am speaking of a criminal gang, ruthless, dangerous men who put their dubious talents at the service of terrorist groups, illegal arms dealers, and the drug trade. There. I've given you some hints about the men in the private cemetery at Grace Hall. That's all I know, and that's all I can tell you.'

Glyn rose to go, but Mr Milczarek gave a rueful sigh, and motioned to him to sit down again.

'I'm going to tell you a story, Mr Edwards,' he said. 'Like all stories, it's a work of fiction, so there's no need for you to make notes. And if you invite me to tell it to anyone else, I'll say that I don't know what you're talking about.

'Once upon a time, in Poland, there existed a merciless gang of criminals who made a large fortune by supplying weapons to terrorist groups operating in the Middle East. These weapons were sometimes bought quite legally from international arms dealers, but sometimes they were stolen from military armouries with ruthless loss of life. Well-planned raids took place in Germany, and in Ukraine. They operated on the "cell" system, so that it was extremely difficult for them to be unmasked. They had no fixed headquarters, but moved from town to town, country to country.

'These seven men controlled a network of over a hundred hired mercenaries, men who would do anything for money. They reported for duty when called upon to do so, and after they'd done the Seven's bidding, they'd merge back into civil society. Many of them are still alive, living happy and prosperous lives in their luxurious houses.'

'How do you know all this, Mr Milczarek?'

'Know all what? Didn't I tell you that this was only a story?

'And then, in the 1980s, the dying years of the Soviet Union, when central control was weakening, they began to consolidate their operations in satellite countries. At the same time, they expanded into the lucrative business of money laundering. And it was then that they began to cause concern to a very rich international financier, a man who had willingly placed himself in the hands of the Chinese Government as their chief enabler in Europe.

'The Polish gang's activities were unsettling the status quo that he had grown comfortable with, so the very rich international financier decided that they would have to be stopped. It was a brave and very dangerous decision to make, but the man in my story was unimaginably rich, and his money made people talk. Are you enjoying this story, Mr Edwards? Because that's all it is, you know: a story.'

'It's very interesting, Mr Milczarek,' said Glyn. 'Maybe you'll have it published someday. So what happened next?'

'The financier had had dealings with the Gang of Seven before and knew them all. So he invited them to a secret conference in the country where he lived. It was to be an intensely private affair, and he insisted that they should come without their usual bodyguards. That should have alerted them that they were in for trouble, but he was offering them deals worth over a billion pounds and had made the brilliant decision to advance them several hundred thousand, which had already passed into their banks through the usual money-laundering channels.'

'So they came?'

'They did, and when they arrived at his secluded retreat, they were immediately beaten unconscious and then shot in the head. It was a sudden, astute solution to the problem of the Gang of Seven. They were all secretly buried, and nothing more would have been heard about them had not some land improvements in the area brought their bodies to light. And that's the end of the story, as far as my inventiveness goes. If you want to finish it, you'll have to make up the rest yourself.'

'How do you know all this?' Glyn asked, and then, as Milczarek's face clouded over, added hurriedly, 'I mean, how do you come up with your ideas?'

'No crime is ever committed completely unseen, Sergeant. There are always servants, pilots, attendants. Collateral damage, sometimes.'

Mr Milczarek stood undecided for a moment, then took his wallet from an inside pocket and extracted a faded black-and-white photograph, which he handed to Glyn.

'That is my brother, Henryk,' he said. 'He, too, was a victim of the Polish gangs. He was a sergeant in the detective police in Warsaw, who got too near a particularly lethal gang boss in Szczecin. Henryk was found floating in the River Oder. He had been shot in the back. His killer was never found. And that's partly why I occasionally make up these stories, like the one I've just told you about the Gang of Seven.'

* * *

'I want to get back into the investigation,' said Lance Middleton. 'Noel Greenspan and Chloe McArthur have already given you an update on all their work for Lydia Gillette, including Chloe's find of those two passports in that house in Newcastle, one British, the other French, both made out in the name of Donald Wainwright. Why France? What did Louis Gillette propose to do there? I know someone in Paris who may have the answer to that question, and I'm flying out there to consult him. But you want to delve further into that business of the Polish exiles, Glyn. Well, I can put you in touch with a man at the security service who knows all about it. I'm sure he'll give you all the help he can.'

DS Glyn Edwards had travelled up to London to consult Lance Middleton in his chambers in Lincoln's Inn. Mr Milczarek's cryptic 'story' about the Gang of Seven had seized his imagination, and he knew that Lance had all kinds of connections in Government departments.

'May I counsel you to be very careful?' said Lance. 'These things have ramifications, as I know to my cost. There have been a lot of puppets in this case, Glyn, people who thought they were movers and shakers, but were in fact controlled by someone very determined who was pulling all the strings. If you work too openly, that someone will send his assassin after you.'

'I belong to a big gang, too,' said DS Edwards stoutly. 'There are many thousands of men and women in my particular gang, and in the end, we'll prove to be more than a match for — well, for the particular puppet master in question. I wish you every success in Paris, Lance. Meanwhile, I'd welcome your letter of introduction to your contact in the secret service.'

* * *

The man who lived in the half-ruined hunting lodge had packed his bags and had already overseen the despatch of his heavier luggage to Euston. He'd found a tenant for the lodge, a widowed schoolmaster who was something of a bird watcher, who had promised to keep the property in decent repair while he was away. He'd sometimes thought of having the ruined part of the old lodge repaired but had grown rather fond of the dilapidated side of the building, overgrown with masses of weeds that flowered purple in the summertime.

His chief client was beginning to lose his nerve. There had been too many assassinations, which offended his sense of decorum. He was not a cheap thug, but an artist in his own way, a man who had once managed an analytical laboratory for a major manufacturing company. Poison was his forte, particularly the use of the various types of cyanide for quick and deadly results.

He had met that kind of desperate overkill before, and it had always preceded some catastrophic fall. Well, he would make himself scarce until the crisis was over.

He had rather admired his client's own foray into the business of elimination and had coached him very carefully in how to carry it out — the holdall, the wine glasses, the bottle of Lauretier Fils brandy, and the obviously forged suicide note. That had not been meant to fool anyone: it was an assassination, pure and simple, a means employed by his client to terrify his debtors into coughing up what they owed him. He had done it very well. A pity that some other fool should have blundered in and altered the scenario for his own trivial ends.

But now, something was driving his client desperate, and he had no intention of branding himself a mass killer. It was time to move on.

* * *

'It's like building a house of cards,' said Michael Brandt, Lance Middleton's contact at the security service. 'Pull away one card, and the whole house collapses. There are times when we have to leave a dangerous character at large because to remove them from circulation could have even more dangerous consequences — dangerous in an international context. And that's why the Gang of Seven were recreated by us as seven Polish political exiles.'

'How did you manage that?' asked Glyn Edwards.

'We allowed Tauber to bribe one of our top civil servants to fake seven identities for the seven men he'd murdered, with a great deal of cooperation from the secret service. They're very good at forging false papers. The bodies had been uncovered by local authority contractors, and your man moved very quickly to mask the truth.'

'So he had a corrupt contact in the security services? Someone he could bribe?'

Michael Brandt smiled and shook his head.

'When you came here this morning, Sergeant Edwards, you were made to sign the Official Secrets Act, which you did entirely of your own free will. The clerk who witnessed your signature explained the significance of what you had done and told you of the grave consequences of revealing any part of our conversation to a third party without our express permission.

'So now I can explain to you that the "corrupt official" was an MI5 agent, who had been briefed to grant various little favours to your man over the course of a number of years. Agents of that kind are known as "sleepers". It was all a long time ago, Sergeant, and that particular sleeper is long dead. But Tauber made the mistake of many of his kind: he thought that he could buy anything with money. And so we were able to monitor just about any of his activities without him ever knowing.'

'He went on to order more killings,' said Glyn. 'Just last month he's murdered at least four people, all of them civilians. Why have you allowed him to get away with it?'

'Because we have to look at a larger picture. This man is deeply involved in the funding of projects dear to some of the emerging European powers, and in recent years to Communist China. Everything he does is under close observation. He has raised massive loans for clients in Ukraine and

China, and it's true to say that he has become essential for the successful operation of their foreign policies. And so he has gone unpunished, because of the greater picture.'

Michael Brandt was a slightly built, bespectacled man, nondescript in appearance, but Glyn Edwards could sense that he was in fact a man with great authority and power. They were sitting in his office in the grand SIS building on Millbank that housed the offices of MI5 and MI6.

'Yes,' Brandt continued, 'we've left him alone, but there are signs that his authority with his international clients is starting to slip. We have a man planted in his house who thinks that he's going soft. He's no longer young, and he's started to bluster and threaten. Our friends down the road have been steadily compiling a dossier of his weaknesses, and when the time's right, they'll leak its contents to the Ukrainian and Chinese Embassies. So if you want you can wait for us to act, or go your own way. It's up to you.'

'This man has committed or authorised a string of vile murders,' said Glyn. 'So if you don't mind, Mr Brandt, I'll go my own policeman's way in bringing him to justice. But I'm very grateful for all that you've told me, and if you get to him before I do, well, there'll be no harm done.'

* * *

'You were right to come to me, Monsieur Lance,' said Maître Lacoste. 'In my particular corner of the Department of Justice we keep a vigilant eye on passport forgers.'

Maître Lacoste had long ago left active service in the French judiciary and lived in retirement in an apartment that gave him a dramatic view of the Basilica of the Sacré Coeur in Montmartre, but he was often called upon unofficially by his former colleagues. Lacoste was one of those functionaries of the law who have the gift of forging friendships of a sort with people on the wrong side of the law.

'This man calling himself Donald Wainwright — you say his real name was Louis Gillette — obtained this passport that you mailed to me from a skilled forger whom I happen to know quite well, so I called upon him, and we had a little chat. This Wainwright had already begun the purchase of a very nice apartment out at Fontainebleau, using that false name. He intended to settle there, and according to my forger friend he had opened an account with the Credit Lyonnais. *Enfin*, he suddenly disappeared, and all these activities were suspended. You tell me that he was, in fact, murdered in England. *Quel dommage!*'

'And there the matter rests,' said Lance. 'An apartment in Fontainebleau . . . So all along he meant to leave Lydia behind.'

'Lydia?'

'His wife.'

'Ah! That, no!' cried Maître Lacoste. 'My forger friend told me — we were sitting here, on this balcony, sharing a bottle of wine — he told me that this Monsieur Wainwright was in high spirits at the thought of starting a new life. He'd left a false trail behind him in Newcastle, and had made two brief visits to France. Did he not tell his wife? For he told my forger friend that as soon as he was settled, he was going to send for her.'

'I shall tell her that,' said Lance. 'It will be some comfort to her, I should think.'

Secretly he thought, *The man must have been insane to think that he'd get away with it. As soon as his father-in-law, Simon Bolt, got wind of it, he'd have been out there with his money and his influence to bring Louis back to England and to his senses.* It was a pity, perhaps, that that had not happened. It might have brought Louis and Lydia together again . . . But no. Louis was into criminal money laundering up to his neck. Poor, erring Lydia was well rid of him.

11. DANGEROUS RUMOURS

'So, Buckley,' said Simon Bolt, 'I've got all my money back — all of it — little thanks to you! No, it's by courtesy of a man I've never heard of, who apparently does that kind of thing as a hobby.'

Buckley, Bolt's chief accountant, looked and felt like an errant schoolboy hauled up before the headmaster. It had been his fault entirely. He had grown too complacent, too sure of himself. Well, he'd been summoned to Chelsea, presumably to get his comeuppance. Better resign before he was sacked.

'I'm very sorry for what happened,' he said, 'and I've brought a letter of resignation with me—'

'Resignation be damned!' Bolt's harsh voice rose to something like a shriek. 'You're too valuable for me to let you go. But don't hire casual labour in future. If you need more help in your practice, get someone to give you a recommendation, and when you get this person, bring him or her here so that I can add my judgement to yours. Now, as to that load of Government paper that Mr Tauber gave me — have you put it to market yet?'

'Yes, Mr Bolt. It's already moving round the City, and I'll have a written memo for you by tomorrow morning. It's quite nice stuff, but it won't yield you much beyond two and a quarter per cent. It's really good of you—'

'Yes, well never mind all that. Have you made that transfer of six million to Mr Tauber's holding account? It's going to pay seven per cent, so he tells me.'

Buckley was silent, his eyes fixed on the carpet. He was standing with Simon Bolt in the parlour of the house in Chelsea.

'Well, have you? Or did you forget?'

'No, I didn't forget. But I was in Frankfurt last week, and a man I know there whispered in my ear that — that Mr Tauber was unsound.'

'What man was this?'

'Rudi Bergmuller, the chief accountant at Bergmann Brothers. He reminded me that the Deutsche Bank's trading rose forty per cent in the second quarter of this year, so they were only too eager to lend some of it out at profit, but he knew, from a friend he has there, that they politely refused Mr Tauber accommodation. And that's why I've not yet made that transfer. I realise you're not sure of my advice at the moment, but I would suggest you either wait for a week or two or tell Mr Tauber that you've changed your mind.'

Simon Bolt had gone very quiet. He sat down in a chair beside the fireplace, unconsciously biting the side of his thumb. Then he looked up, and smiled.

'You can see now, Buckley, why I won't give you the sack, which you so richly deserve! You know too many interesting things. I summoned you here today to give you a telling-off, but in the light of what you've told me, I'd like you to stay to lunch, if you will. There are other things that we can discuss.'

'You're very kind, Mr Bolt,' said Buckley. 'As always, I am entirely at your service. I wonder whether you might drop a hint to London Tower Investments? They've been very kind to us over the years, but I know that they have a very large sum invested in Mr Tauber's European projects.'

Simon Bolt thought, *This is how business crashes start — rumours that are passed on, often by word of mouth, mushrooming into a monstrous denunciation and a spectacular fall.* Manfred had been his friend for half a lifetime, but where financial stability and safety were concerned, not to speak of the safety of his widowed daughter, friendship went only so far.

* * *

Manfred Tauber's party for his clients went ahead as arranged. Grace Hall seemed to be filled with young men in black trousers and white shirts, and lively, smiling girls in dark frocks and white aprons. These workers were supplied by Mayfair Cuisine of Chichester, who had provided a magnificent luncheon buffet in the main parlour. Later, afternoon tea would be served, before the guests made their way home. Williams and his own domestic staff were only too happy to keep out of sight, as the caterers insisted on total control of the proceedings.

Corinne looked superb in a clinging white dress from one of the Paris fashion houses. She had agreed to wear the ruby necklace and matching earrings that he had bought her for her last birthday. It was getting too chilly for comfort in England now. Perhaps they would go to Cannes for the whole of December, and into the New Year.

Of the fifty guests, twelve were Tauber's own customers, the people who always adjourned to his library to buy an antique book or two. All of them knew that they had no option but to take what he offered them, and pay the price demanded.

He smiled to himself. None of them probably opened a book from one year to another, but by sticking to this arrangement they could spirit away large sums of money to bank accounts abroad without fear of detection. A man could buy a book for ten thousand pounds, and would be given a receipt, but his money would end up secure and tax free in an obscure bank in Switzerland, France, or Germany, or, if they wished it, in Lebanon.

Over the years, he had bound these men to himself with terror. They were all moderately prosperous businessmen who had allowed him to syphon off and launder millions for them in unpaid tax. So they came faithfully, twice a year, to buy more books, but now they were forced to give him the money that he required under threat of being reported to the Inland Revenue. In other words, they were a useful source of quite considerable supplementary income.

From time to time, he would drop hints that one or other of his many accountants might have a sudden stab of conscience and confess all to the authorities. His hints were framed as jokes, but they all knew that they were, in fact, threats.

A few weeks earlier, one of his clients, Louis Gillette, the son-in-law of his old business partner Simon Bolt, had begun to make preparations to flee abroad, throwing in his lot with Samuel Harker, a fellow gallery owner, who was also a very successful money launderer. Gillette had defrauded his father-in-law of a million pounds and looked like getting away with it. Well, Gillette had proved to be a bird ripe for the plucking.

From early in the year, he had noticed that some of his 'bibliophile' clients were making grumbling noises, straining at the bit, and he had feared that they were going to call his bluff. After all, to expose them would be to expose himself. But he had taken exceptional measures, and the threat of Louis Gillette had been removed.

It had been an intensely exciting business, but the strain of it had told afterwards. It was just after that adventure that the headaches had begun, headaches that had affected his vision. His doctor had been noncommittal, putting everything down to 'advanced years'. Damn it all, he was hardly decrepit! Perhaps he needed a younger, more go-ahead physician. His friend Simon Bolt swore by his young doctor. He would contrive to forget all about the elimination of Louis Gillette. In the meantime, it had brought his grumbling 'bibliophiles' to heel.

The other guests were some of the great and the good of Oldminster, including the Lord Mayor, Edward Billington, and his deputy, Jimmy Parle, both looking delighted to be there, and accompanied by their wives, both vivid blondes of an uncertain age, clutching glasses and chattering away. There were a couple of head teachers, a gaggle of lawyers, and Superintendent Philpot, resplendent in his dress uniform. It would be as well to butter him up, as one of his officers, Sergeant Edwards, was proving to be a bit of a nuisance.

The buffet was going well, and soon he'd be able to take himself off to the library, to help his tame bibliophiles choose some more books. Corinne would enjoy being hostess. At the moment she was gazing up into the eyes of a rather handsome young man who was talking animatedly about something or other. Well, let her have her bit of fun.

He sensed that something was amiss as soon as he entered the library. His twelve clients were all standing in a huddle at the far end of the book-lined room. They stopped speaking to each other as they saw him. A few of them, clients of long standing, looked abashed and subdued, but among the younger men, he could see something like defiance.

'Well, gentlemen,' said Tauber, 'it's time to choose your books, and then we can agree a price. I'm hoping that, between you, we can come up with a total of a hundred and twenty thousand pounds. Something like that.'

He heard the sound of uncertain laughter, and felt a tightness in his stomach. One of the younger ones, James Elder stepped forward. He had evidently been chosen as some kind of spokesperson. He ran an import/export business in Birmingham, and Manfred Tauber knew him to be deeply corrupt.

'Well, you know, Mr Tauber,' said Elder, 'we've decided to give your kind offer a miss this month. There's a rumour going the rounds that the Deutsche Bank has refused you accommodation. They're talking about that on the Stock Exchange. So if you don't mind, we'll give the antique books a miss on this occasion, and just enjoy your very kind hospitality.'

There was an insolence in the young man's tone that chilled him to the bone. Credit was the most valuable commodity any businessman could have. Without it, nothing else mattered. If your credit was compromised, your holdings became meaningless figures on spreadsheets. Nothing beyond the doors of the Bank of England was backed up by gold bullion, and even that reassuring fact was not necessarily true nowadays.

'Very well, gentlemen,' he said calmly. 'I'm sorry that you've been listening to baseless rumours, but that is your decision. By all means enjoy the rest of the day.'

'There's just one more thing, Mr Tauber,' said James Elder. 'We brought you a little present as a token of our appreciation. Mr Goretti?'

Mario Goretti stepped forward, a man whom he'd forced to pay twenty-six thousand pounds for a Graham Greene novel. On that occasion he had almost fainted with fear, the monitory death of Louis Gillette clearly on his mind. Today, though, he was clearly half drunk, nodding and smiling in some kind of vilely arrogant triumph. He was holding a bottle, which he thrust unceremoniously into Tauber's hand.

It was a bottle of Lauretier Fils Grande Amber Peach Brandy.

* * *

That evening, when there was only a glimmer of daylight across the rear gardens, Manfred Tauber, emerging from one of his headaches, thought that he saw Louis Gillette standing beside the ornamental fountain that had been turned off for the winter. But no, he must be seeing things. What were those lines from Macbeth? *Duncan is in his grave/ After life's fitful fever he sleeps well.*

When he looked out from his bedroom window an hour later, Louis Gillette was still there.

* * *

Early the next morning, Oleg Yanukovych, Undersecretary at the Ukrainian Interior Ministry, left Boryspill Airport for the long haul to Beijing. His government had been mesmerised by the reputedly enormous wealth of Manfred Tauber, as other governments had been in the past by the tycoons of yesteryear. Some, of course, like the Rothschilds, 'moneylenders to kings and princes', had proved to be valuable allies in the funding of projects in the nineteenth century, but others had been shaky, to say the least, and some small European countries had emerged gasping with relief after disentangling themselves from the clutches of dishonest brokers.

Well, Ukraine, said to be the poorest country in Europe, was not going to be caught out. The rumours had started in Frankfurt, and then had spread rapidly to the other major bourses of Europe. The smooth-talking 'broker's broker' was said to be unsound, his vast wealth a paper fantasy.

And then had come the secret dossier from the British Foreign Office, more or less confirming Tauber's empire to be nothing more than a paper confection. The British courier, who had met him secretly in Kyiv, had told him that a copy of the dossier had been sent to his opposite number in Beijing. It was time to disengage, and to broker an immediate rapprochement on the matter with the People's Republic of China.

The President had been quite specific in his instructions. Tauber and his like were no longer to be entrusted with the funding of great state enterprises, like the gas pipeline. Let the project be funded by the treasuries of the respective nations, even if it meant raising taxes, and making economies elsewhere. China was one of the world's great powers, and a firm alliance with Beijing would bring China in as a realistic guarantor of Ukraine's independence in the face of possible Russian aggression. He himself had been mesmerised by Tauber's smooth talk. It was time to wake up to immediate realities.

* * *

'I'm beginning to think that it's time for me to broaden my horizons,' said John Williams, the house manager at Grace

Hall. He was sitting on a bench in the private cemetery, talking to Danny O'Toole, the morose gardener. He had been cutting back some of the overgrowth in the cemetery around the first Mrs Tauber's tomb when Williams had joined him.

'Why? Why would you want to do that? You've got a cushy billet here, John.'

'You used to tell me that he was going soft,' said Williams, 'and I thought you were exaggerating. But the other day one of those sneaking "bibliophiles" stood up to him and answered back, and he did nothing about it. Just a few years ago he would have. But he did nothing about it.'

'He's getting old,' said O'Toole. 'Maybe he just wants a quiet life.'

'You've heard the rumours, haven't you? He's supposed to be on the blink.'

'And you're going to be one of the rats that desert the sinking ship?'

'I'm a trained house manager, Danny, and good at the job. There are still wealthy folk in England who'd be eager to give me a job if I left here. But if various official nosey parkers come sniffing round here at Grace Hall, I don't want to be here. I think I've been too loyal, and it's made me blind to Mr Tauber's faults, and to the fact that he's starting to become senile.'

'You're exaggerating.'

'No, I'm not. And a man like that, a man who's made away with people, could be very dangerous if he suddenly goes over the edge. And I've got a record, Danny. Oh, I was never a great villain, but it was bad enough that I did time when I was younger.'

'I didn't know that, John. Sorry to hear it.'

'Anyway, Corrine's becoming unsettled, and although she's been a true wife to Mr Tauber, she's a shrewd woman when all's said and done, and I think she might find consolation elsewhere. She likes loads of money, and jewels, and frocks from Paris. And she's always had an eye for handsome young men. Compared to Mr Tauber, she's only a girl. She bought a huge diamond brooch from Asprey's, and I happen to know that she sold it on at a profit. Soon, Danny, she may go walkabout.'

'So you're thinking of handing in your notice?'

'I want to get myself secure in a new job before the balloon bursts here. Since that man Goretti stood up to him, he's not been himself. He's — he's seeing things, and talking to himself. I think his brain's turned. You know the little summer house at the back of the formal garden? Well, he had me put a writing desk in there, and he goes there, now, most days.'

'What's he doing in there?'

'I peeped through the window once, and saw him frantically writing away at something or other. It looked like one of those A4 diaries. The place was full of old broken garden tools and other junk, but he wouldn't let me clear them out. He never raises his voice, as you know, but he did then. "Leave things alone!" he said, quite sharpish. "Just do what I tell you!" He had me put a new lock on the door and kept both keys. By rights, he would have given one to me, but I could see he was in no mood for argument.'

'Well, I'm stopping here until somebody sacks me. But I wish you all the best, John. I'd better finish this job, then it'll be time to have a bite to eat.'

O'Toole watched John Williams leave the cemetery, and then took out his smart phone. He stood in front of the first Mrs Tauber's tomb and waited while various connections were made.

'Mr Brandt? I need to speak to one of your folk urgently. Tauber's beginning to break, and it's time for us to bring in the police — plain clothes, of course. I know you've got firm contacts with some officers in the Oldshire Police. Can you meet me tomorrow morning at the Grapes? It's a pub just outside the Hall gates. We can talk in the pub garden.'

* * *

'I got here at seven this morning,' said Michael Brandt. 'There are very good trains from London to Oldminster.

Now, what did you mean by saying that Manfred Tauber's beginning to break?'

'I think age, and his conscience, such as it is, are catching up with him,' said Danny O'Toole. 'Williams says he's started to see things, and he's talking to himself. A man of that type losing his faculties can be very dangerous.'

'His empire may be on the brink of collapse, O'Toole, but that's not going to bring him to account for the murders he's committed. Oh, why pretend otherwise? He's removed anyone who stood in his way, either personally or through an unknown assassin. Edmund Salis, who talked too much, Samuel Harker, the crooked art dealer and money launderer who posed a threat to his own operations, and Charles Deacon, another weak link in the chain who could have been intimidated into telling all he knew, if Tauber hadn't got there first. And then, the murder of Louis Gillette. The senior detective here, DI French, reckons that was a personal score to settle, and that Tauber carried out the killing himself.'

'What kind of personal score?'

'French believes that Tauber did it to avenge his old friend Simon Bolt, who'd been defrauded out of a small fortune by Gillette. We're convinced that Bolt knew nothing about that. And of course, Gillette was entangled with Samuel Harker, who was one of Tauber's rivals in the business of money laundering.'

'Would Mr Tauber really have carried out Gillette's "execution" personally?'

'Why not? Remember the seven Poles whom he massacred in the eighties. He's never been averse to a spot of murder.'

'But we've no direct proof of his complicity in any of these cyanide murders.'

'No, we haven't, and I think Tauber knows it. Oh, he may very well go bust, but busted financiers always seem to have plenty left to live upon very comfortably. So why did you ask me to come down here today?'

'Tauber's suddenly taken to locking himself away in a little summer house, where Williams has seen him writing some kind of diary. He's had a new lock put on the door, and no one's allowed in there, not even me — it's where I store some of my garden tools. I think it's time for someone to nose around in there and see what Tauber's up to.'

'Hm . . . What kind of security does he have?'

'There are six bodyguards, three for the daytime, and three for the night shift.'

'Right. Give me a couple of days for me to set various things in motion, and then we'll see if we can't unlock the secrets of the summer house. These bodyguards . . . Are they based here permanently, or do they travel with him?'

'They travel with him.'

'Then find out a day when he'll be away from home, and we'll take a closer look at that summer house. How many domestic staff are there?'

'Six. There's Williams, two resident maids, and three part-time cleaners. Only Williams is privy to Tauber's various secrets. How are you going to do this, Mr Brandt?'

'Well, there'll be no cloak-and-dagger stuff. Once we've decided on the right day, a senior officer from Oldshire Police will ring up Grace Hall, and inform them that intruders have penetrated the grounds, and may have concealed themselves in the house. An immediate search will be made, with or without Williams's cooperation.'

'He'll cooperate, sir. He's already convinced that he's standing on the deck of a sinking ship.'

'Good. As I said, it will be an open operation, conducted by uniformed police. They'll be accompanied by Detective Sergeant Edwards, who's been involved in all this business from the beginning, and one of my people, posing as a detective inspector. A chap called Fuller. He's there to tell Williams whatever lies he deems necessary, thus sparing the blushes of the real police officers.'

'This summer house, sir — Williams doesn't have a key. Tauber made a point of not giving him the duplicate, which a house manager would expect to be given.'

'No problem there, O'Toole. My man Fuller can open any lock you present to him.

'Finally, at the right time, we'll jam cellular signals and cut the phone lines and internet for Grace Hall — that'll cut the place off just in case Williams or anybody else decides to alert Tauber. As soon as you can find out a day when Manfred Tauber is away from home, all these measures will be put into action.'

'I'm very impressed, sir. As you know, I've been a "sleeper" here for more time than I care to remember, and after this I hope I'll be assigned to something quite different. I'm a bit tired of playing the gruff backwoodsman. Are you prepared to grant me a request as part of my pay-off?'

'That depends on what the request is.'

'It's Williams, sir. He knows a lot about Manfred Tauber, things going back for years, but as far as I can make out, he's never been someone holding the gun, or pouring poison down people's throats. Are you prepared to leave him alone once this business is settled?'

'I see. You've grown fond of him, and that may be clouding your judgement. But I'll bear in mind what you say, and if there's a way of letting Williams off the hook, I'll let you know.'

'What do you think we'll find in the summer house?'

'All we know is what you've told me: he's writing something — maybe it's instructions to people we don't know about, or maybe he suddenly fancies himself as a novelist, and is locking himself away there until he produces his magnum opus. We'll find out, won't we, once we've bluffed our way into his secret den.'

12. A TRYING DAY IN THE CITY

Manfred Tauber left Grace Hall for London in his Bentley early in the morning. He had given his three bodyguards the day off. He preferred this mode of travel to the train, as it meant he could visit several people while in London without having to hail taxis. His chauffeur, Monkton, was one of those men who seemed able to park anywhere.

He had taken great care over his appearance, dressing in one of his more expensive Savile Row suits, and wearing the pearl-grey Homburg hat that was by way of being one of his trademarks. Today, he intended to go to the top. These rumours would have to be quashed before an unimaginable disaster occurred. He would seek an immediate interview with the Governor of the Bank of England and propose that he should deposit with him his American currency holding of twelve million dollars. Then he would go to Lloyds and confer with one or two of the 'names', seeking support for what he would call a minor blip in his investment programme.

He would then call unannounced at the Ukrainian Embassy, where he knew that the commercial attaché would be overawed by his easy but forceful manner, enough to make him cable Yanukovych to exercise caution. Finally, he would call on Rothschild's in St Swithin's Lane, fixedly and seek their vocal support in order to tide him over a rather tricky patch. Yes, that's what he'd call it: a rather tricky patch. A good word from Rothschild's would go a long way to ensuring that his paper empire remained comparatively undisturbed.

He had seen Louis Gillette again, late on the previous evening. Corinne was somewhere in London, he didn't know where, and it had frightened him to see his victim again, standing in the shade of the grand staircase, looking reproachful. He didn't believe in ghosts. Whatever was conjuring up this vision of Louis Gillette must be some kind of abnormality of the brain. When this crisis was over, he'd go to see someone in Harley Street who could make a sane and sober evaluation of his physical state.

Oh, Magda! Do you remember the excitement of our early days together? I was full of promise, then. Now, I'm nothing more than a hollow shell, a husk.

* * *

'Mr Williams? I am Detective Inspector Fuller of the Oldshire Constabulary. We have reason to believe that there are intruders on this property, probably lying low in the grounds, and we're here to flush them out.'

'Intruders? Do you mean burglars?'

'I can't tell you more at this juncture, for security reasons. All I can say is that Mr Manfred Tauber is a very prominent financier, who has made enemies both here and abroad. There are six uniformed officers now searching the grounds, and I must ask all indoor staff to stay here, in the main house, until the search is concluded.'

John Williams thought, *Do as the man says, and keep out of the spotlight.*

'Very well, sir. We'll do as you say. How long do you think the search will take?'

'Can't say just yet. I'll let you know as soon as we have them.'

Fuller hurried away in the direction of the formal garden. Looking out of the parlour window, Williams could see a number of uniformed figures moving between the trees. And who was that? Sergeant Edwards, the policeman who liked to discuss his boss's taste in brandy. He'd had a bit of a cheek, asking Mr Tauber impertinent questions.

Williams retreated to his pantry, where he tried to put through a call to Tauber's London solicitor, but the line was down. Perhaps the intruders had cut the wire? His boss had a lot of enemies — real enemies, killers, for want of a better word. Maybe he was about to desert the sinking ship, but he'd no intention of pushing the captain off the bridge. Using his smart phone, he tried to call Tauber directly, but there was no signal.

* * *

Manfred Tauber's chauffeur parked the Bentley in an alley near Threadneedle Street, and the financier walked the short distance to the Bank of England. He was always received with deference, usually by the deputy governor, and he saw no reason why he should be treated any differently on this occasion. He had brought with him the necessary transfers for him to deposit twelve million dollars with the bank, as a boost to their dollar reserves. That money, thank goodness, was guaranteed by the Chase Manhattan Bank: it was real money, not yet another product of creative accountancy.

Depositing that money would dissipate any doubts about his financial probity, after which he would turn his attention to tightening the screws on his rebellious 'bibliophiles'. And in particular, he would make an example of Mario Goretti, the insolent restaurateur who had dared to question his absolute authority over them by giving him a bottle of Lauretier Fils brandy. Damn him, what had he meant by that? He would arrange with his man in the half-ruined hunting lodge to serve Goretti a very special glass of brandy that he wouldn't like.

He was courteously received by the bank reception and asked to wait a few moments while enquiries were made as to the availability that morning of the governor or the deputy governor. He waited by himself, sitting on a polished bench, watching all kinds of busy people coming and going.

After a quarter of an hour, he was approached by a smiling young man in a dark business suit wearing an Eton tie, who shook hands, and led him into a remote office on the ground floor. The young man sat behind a bare desk, and motioned Tauber to take the only other seat in the room.

'I'm David Steiner, clerk accountant to the chief cashier. Everybody else is very busy this morning. How may I help you?'

Who was this fellow? Why had he not been taken directly to the deputy governor? Well, better get down to business. He opened his briefcase and placed a folder on the desk.

'I wish to deposit this order of transfer for twelve million dollars with the bank, in order to boost your dollar holdings at this time. I'm a very busy man, Mr er — Steiner, so if you'll give me a signed receipt, I'll be on my way.'

The young man lounged back in his chair and looked out of the window for a moment.

'It's very kind of you to make the offer, Mr Tauber, but at the moment we're not in need of any augmentation of our dollar holdings. Why not go down to the Stock Exchange, and try your luck on the money market? I must go. I'm wanted upstairs at any moment.'

Tauber left the Bank of England and told his chauffeur to drive him to the Stock Exchange.

* * *

'As easy,' said Fuller, the security service man posing as a police inspector, 'as taking sweets off a baby. Locks on summerhouse doors are no challenge at all.' He pushed open the door, and he and Glyn Edwards entered Manfred Tauber's secret retreat. Outside, the other uniformed officers were making a show of searching the grounds for the fictional intruders.

'Let's search through all this rubbish before we look at the desk,' said Glyn.

It was a dusty, gloomy place, with a pile of spades and hoes leaning against the far wall. There were a couple of battered tea chests, which seemed to be full of junk, things probably saved in case they would 'come in handy' at some unspecified time in the future.

DS Edwards reached down into one of the chests, and pulled out a dusty blue canvas holdall, with tan leather handles. If a witness statement was to be believed, the killer of Louis Gillette had carried an identical holdall. He would take it back with him to Jubilee House, where Forensics would run some tests.

'Have you found anything, Mr Fuller?'

'I've found a pair of good-quality black suede gloves in this corner. Seems an odd sort of thing to chuck away among the rubbish.'

A picture was forming in DS Edwards's mind: a heavily built man in a dark coat, and perhaps wearing suede gloves, carrying a blue holdall with tan handles, opening the door of Louis Gillette's gallery, the figure glimpsed by Eleanor Fox, the observant bookseller from the King's Arcade. Even at that stage of the investigation, he was reluctant to draw the obvious conclusion.

'Let's see what's in the desk, now, Mr Fuller. Oh, that's locked, too.'

'No problem.' Fuller produced a set of pick-locks, and opened the desk drawer. Glyn reminded himself that this man was not, in fact, a police officer, but a member of the security service.

The drawer contained an A4 diary for 2018, the kind of diary often bought by offices and businesses of all kinds. There were also a number of cheap ballpoint pens. Glyn opened it at the first page and saw that it was being used as a writing book, with some kind of narrative continuing across the spaces provided for the various months and weeks. He sat down at the desk and began to read.

The 'Confession' of Manfred Tauber.

It was towards the end of August this year that I determined to show the more timid of my clients that I was not a man to be trifled with. Well into my seventies, I felt that my iron grip over my vast financial empire was starting to slip. I was losing the power of concentration, and even my own staff were whispering among themselves that I was losing my grip. How wrong they were! A stern warning would bring the weaker brethren to heel. Vast financial edifices like mine rely on trust to continue successfully. Once people begin to question you too closely about your assets, you could be on the road to ruin. So I had to bring my clientele to heel by frightening them into compliance.

I was thinking in particular of the men I like to call the 'bibliophiles', who furnish me with a steady income a couple of times a year by buying books from me as a means of spiriting away large sums of money to secret accounts abroad. For years they were delighted with the arrangements, but as real money became tighter after the crash of 2008, I began to turn the screw: what had been voluntary on their part became compulsory. They didn't like it, but they had to put up with it.

In the past, I had employed what I had better call 'professional help' to get rid of embarrassments that stood in my way. I had a long-standing agreement with a man whose name I shall not reveal, who would rid me of certain inconvenient people for a fee — a massive fee, but worth every penny. If the 'bibliophiles' became too strident, then one or other of them would be visited by my 'professional help'.

But there was somebody else whom I determined to deal with myself. My helper would show me what to do, and I would do it. It was personal, you see.

Why am I writing all this? This account will never see the light of day. Well, earlier this year, I began a course of therapy with a psychiatrist who has a very expensive practice off Harley Street. I told him of my increased feelings of insecurity, and a growing suspicion that I was being spied upon. I only let him see a fraction of my true nature, which was cheating, I suppose, but his advice did some good.

One of the things he strongly advised me to do was to write down, as though it was a story, all that I was doing, and all that I had done. 'Confess all to yourself,' he said, 'and you'll be a long way to forgiving yourself.' That's why I've decided to take his advice, and had Williams clear a space in this summer house for me to work on my 'confession' undisturbed.

So let me explain how I personally killed Louis Gillette, the parasitic son-in-law of my old friend Simon Bolt.

* * *

It had been virtually impossible to see anyone at Lloyd's who mattered. He had been passed from office to office, finally being received by a woman who could scarcely conceal her impatience to be elsewhere. No, this woman told him, it was not now the policy for 'names' to involve themselves as guarantors, not since the crash of 2008. 'I'm not familiar with your contacts here, Mr Tauber,' she'd said, 'but I would suggest that it's not prudent in times like these to go seeking guarantors in this way. It makes people nervous.'

Nervous! Arrogant little fool. She couldn't be more than twenty-five, in her off-the-peg suit and pathetic kitten heels, lecturing him on the rights and wrongs of business practice. He'd get a better reception than that at Rothschild's. But first, he would call at the Ukrainian Embassy, and get them to send a warning to Yanukovych to exercise discretion.

His chauffeur wove his way through the London traffic with an expert's skill and, when they arrived in Holland Park, Kensington, he contrived to stop directly opposite the Ukrainian Embassy. He introduced himself, and the young man at the desk made a brief phone call.

'Yes, Mr Tauber, the undersecretary will see you immediately.'

This was more like it! He was feeling tired and dispirited. It was to be hoped that the undersecretary was not another uppity young man.

He was taken up by lift to the undersecretary's office, and when he entered a smiling man of forty or so rose from his desk to greet him.

'Mr Tauber? Andrei Ponomarenko. Let me take your coat. Vasily, can we have some tea?'

Manfred Tauber gave an inner sigh of relief and relaxed in his chair. The day had started badly, but it looked now as though things were going to improve.

'We've not met before, Mr Tauber,' said the undersecretary, 'but I've heard everything about you, and what you've been doing for my country. You have my thanks. Now, how can I help you today?'

'I had thought to have seen the commercial attaché, who knows me quite well—'

'He's sick this morning, Mr Tauber. That's the term that we use here when someone's nursing a hangover. Sick! But here's the tea. I'll be mother, if that's all right with you. Now, what can I do for you?'

'I want to speak privately to Mr Yanukovych in Kyiv. I was going to ask that you let me speak to him from here, using your private line. I've done this once or twice before. Or failing that, I can write a message for you to despatch to him.'

'Oleg Yanukovych! He's one of the coming men in Ukraine, Mr Tauber, a more dynamic ambassador for my country than chair-bound apparatchiks like me!'

The tea was strong and sweet, and very welcome.

'We all have our parts to play in any great enterprise, Mr Ponomarenko. So will you arrange for me to speak to him now, in Kyiv, on the private line?'

'He's not in Kyiv, Mr Tauber, and at the moment I've no direct means of contacting him. He's in Beijing, sent there on a sort of secret mission by our president.'

'Beijing! He and I have had very close dealings of a financial nature, you see, dealings involving millions of dollars. I'm surprised that he's gone off to China without letting me know first.' *Oh, God! Something was wrong.*

'More tea? Those cream biscuits are quite nice. Yes, he's gone to Beijing to negotiate inter-state funding of our ambitious project for a gas pipeline, and other parallel enterprises. It seems that both Ukraine and China have decided to fund these projects directly from the treasuries of both countries, rather than relying on foreign capital investment. You look nonplussed, Mr Tauber. But that's politics, I'm afraid. Well, you know that. It's always a risk doing business directly with a nation state.

'You won't stay? Well, I'm sorry for that. But you see, China has been a staunch defender of Ukraine, and this move will bind the two nations even closer.'

It was all very civilised, but it was only too apparent that he was being warned off. Yes, he knew all about politics, enough at least to realise that the Bank of England, too, had received instructions from someone not to upset the People's Republic of China.

He took a polite farewell of the undersecretary and made his way back to his car.

'To Rothschild's now, Mr Tauber?'

'No. I'll give Rothschild's a miss today. Take me to the Savoy. I intend to stay in London for the night. You drive back to Grace Hall and meet me tomorrow at the Savoy at eleven o'clock.'

No, he wouldn't bother with Rothschild's. They too, would have received instructions from above not to lend him support.

* * *

I began by despising Louis Gillette, a poseur and dilettante, who knew nothing of art, and less of business. I would meet him at various public functions and would think what an appalling mistake Lydia Bolt had made in marrying him.

It was in the middle of June this year that I heard of Gillette's entanglement with Samuel Harker, a very dangerous money launderer, whose projects more than once presented a danger to the legitimate operation of the money markets. The people I employ to find out these things then discovered that Gillette, with Harker's connivance, had managed to rob his father-in-law of the sum of a million pounds. It was then that my dislike of the man turned to hatred. He was a danger to my friend Simon Bolt, and a danger to me. So I determined that I would personally rid the world of Gillette. I consulted my man in the half-ruined hunting lodge, and he very kindly devised a plan whereby I could carry out the liquidation of Gillette myself. It was many years since I had personally got rid of a whole gang of extortioners by having them bludgeoned to unconsciousness, and then shooting all seven of them myself. Good riddance to bad rubbish. And so I set out to rid the world of Gillette.

He knew me, of course, and was delighted to receive a letter from me, saying that I had heard of his dealings with Samuel Harker, and would like to use his contacts to spirit a large amount of money away to the safety of the continent without HMRC knowing anything about it. I arranged to meet him at the Rembrandt Gallery at 4.30 p.m. on Friday, 14 September, the day when the various businesses in the King's Arcade at Oldminster hold their popular autumn sales. He was to bring my letter with him and surrender it to me.

I arrived on time and manoeuvred my way through the crowd of shoppers thronging the Arcade. I cannot tell you how excited I was! The gallery was empty — of course it was! Who would want to view Gillette's badly chosen collection of daubs on sales day? I turned the OPEN notice on the door round to CLOSED, so that I would not be disturbed. He was waiting for me in the back room of the gallery, smiling and simpering, clearly anxious to hear how I could add to his despicable villainies. He opened his safe and produced my letter from within and handed it back to me. I could see that the safe was otherwise empty — when was the last time he even sold a painting, I wonder?

'I'm so glad we can come to an accommodation,' he said. 'A friend of mine hinted the other week that you were going to murder me! "No choice but murder", you'd told him.'

'Your friend was talking nonsense,' I replied. I knew who that friend would have been. It was the man Samuel Harker, and when I used those words in a conversation I had with him in the Savoy Bar, I was talking about him, not Gillette. Evidently, he thought I had been referring to Louis Gillette, and had warned him accordingly. None of it mattered. They were both dead men in my book.

I can hear myself talking now, as I write this. 'Well, Mr Gillette, this is an auspicious occasion which calls for a little celebration!' I had brought with me a holdall prepared for me by my man in the half-ruined lodge — no, I won't reveal his name. I took from it a bottle of Lauretier Fils Grande Amber Peach Brandy, and two brandy glasses.

I was talking all the time, an endless stream of chat about money markets, the making of fortunes, and the need to seize opportunities when they arose. I watched him nodding his silly head in agreement.

I unscrewed the bottle of brandy and, sitting as far back as I could to avoid the escaping fumes, I filled the two glasses, raised mine aloft, and cried, 'To our successful venture!' Louis Gillette, who was lounging back in his chair, repeated the words, and knocked back his glass of brandy.

He died almost immediately, and in his final convulsion he fell forward across the table. Prussic acid — hydrogen cyanide — has that effect. I sat for a moment exhilarated by my success in ridding the world of this particular parasite and tried to control my almost unendurable excitement. I felt thirty years younger!

But there was more work to do. I quickly screwed the cap back on the brandy bottle and put it back in the holdall.

Following my man's instructions, I drained the two wine glasses down the sink — there was a sort of wash place at the back of the shop — and returned them, too, to the holdall. I must confess that I felt rather squeamish about the next part of the process. I took another, clean, wine glass from the holdall, and moulded Gillette's fingers around it. Bringing out the bottle again, I poured a little of its deadly contents into the new glass and put it near the dead man's hand. I'd thought about leaving the bottle there, too, but thought it better to take it away and get rid of it. After all, it had come from my own cellar, and could possibly have been traced back there. A glass, but no bottle — well, one had to take risks in matters of this nature.

The icing on the cake, as it were, was a suicide note, carefully penned by my man in the half-ruined lodge, which I left on the table. It read: 'I cannot face my creditors. Lydia must not be dragged down by me'. I thought that was rather neat. I looked around and saw that leaving the wine glass upright would suggest that Gillette had had time to put it back on the table, so I tipped it over on to its side. There was talk of a missing cash box, but I know nothing about that.

And in this way I rid the world of a dangerous parasite and a potential enemy. I felt no remorse. Why should I have done? I still don't.

And then a blundering fool called Jack Prosser came long after I had gone and muddied the waters! I have since learnt that Prosser had made Lydia his mistress. Perhaps he, too, is a candidate for the prussic acid treatment.

I left the still crowded Arcade and made my way through back streets, dumping the bottle in a bin behind the fish market, and making my way to the car park by the Town Hall. I was back home in less than half an hour. I hid the holdall here, among all this junk in the summer house. I burnt the letter in the parlour fire grate.

When I've 'unburdened my soul' further, I'll burn all this in the garden incinerator. I'm enjoying recalling all these things and will have other deaths to chronicle. And then

I will take myself off to Harley Street to have my brain looked at. I'm seeing too many visions of Louis Gillette for comfort.

* * *

Manfred Tauber relaxed in the Thames Foyer of the Savoy Hotel, where he had just finished his afternoon tea. A famous product of the hotel, it was served with all the solemnity of a religious ritual. It was worth paying for service of this kind. He would stay here for the rest of the day, until dinner time. After that, he would get a good night's sleep.

He fell into a rather agreeable doze but was suddenly awakened by some people laughing. It was a crowd of young people of the upper class, with the confident arrogance of their caste. That woman looked exactly like Corinne. And the man she was talking to — wasn't that the handsome young fellow who'd been taking a very close interest in her at the 'bibliophiles" party?

Surely that *was* Corinne? The gaggle of young people, still laughing at some private joke, made their way to the exit. Manfred Tauber called over one of the waiters.

'Those people just going out — are they staying in the hotel?'

'No, sir. They just came in for drinks in one of the bars.'

It could have been Corinne. Well, he gave her a long leash. But it was a bit disturbing to see her fraternising with that young man. Corinne was a fixed point in a turning world. Pray God that all was well.

13. THE MAN IN THE HALF-RUINED LODGE

While Manfred Tauber was busying himself in London, the self-styled Detective Inspector Fuller, and the bona fide Detective Sergeant Edwards were still in the summer house, reading Tauber's damning confession.

'How could a man like this,' said Glyn Edwards, 'a colossus of commerce, be so stupid as to leave this confession lying around? He may put quotation marks around the word "Confession", but that's what it is, a confession to having murdered Louis Gillette, among other killings. We can obtain an arrest warrant on the strength of this alone.'

'People like Tauber are so used to having their orders obeyed that they become complacent,' said Fuller. 'No one was to come into this summer house but himself, and nobody did. However curious they would have been, they would all have been terrified to go against his orders. And of course, he had both keys. Let's see what else he has to say.'

I was upset to hear that a vagrant had found the discarded bottle of brandy and had drunk from it. Poor fellow! He had nothing to do with all this, and God knows he had little enough of this world's goods. I sent a substantial (and anonymous) donation to the night shelter for such people in Oldminster, run by the Salvation Army.

Later, I had reason to make my cyanide man work overtime. He didn't like it one bit, and for one rather tense moment I thought I was going to lose the convenience of his services. It was becoming essential to get rid of Samuel Harker, whose money-laundering activities were starting to interfere seriously with projects of my own on the continent. And he was another fellow who was causing trouble for my old friend Simon Bolt. He was a growing danger, and he had to go.

I don't know what tale my man spun when he went to see Harker at his gallery near Westminster Cathedral: he never told me, and I never asked him. Whatever it was, it proved to be successful. He told me that he had taken a small bottle of prussic acid with him, rather than a bottle of brandy, as the brandy manoeuvre had been all over the papers, and various fantastic theories had appeared on the internet. After a certain amount of sweet-talking, Harker had produced a bottle of brandy himself, and a couple of glasses, and my man had used some trick or other to make certain that Harker's tipple was laced with cyanide. So much for Harker! He was no loss to anybody. That was in late September.

I'll skip the next one for the moment and write about the crooked accountant Edmund Salis. Quite simply, he proved to be a blabbermouth who would certainly have involved me in any craven confession that he cared to make. My man got rid of him too. I don't know how he did it, and he seemed disinclined to tell me. By this time, he was getting rather fed up with my constant calls upon his services.

The one death that I have been dreading to 'confess' was that of Charles Deacon. This wretched, unstable man had worked as a clerk in a private bank that I had once owned, but he had since fallen on hard times. I helped him in several ways, but he was not the kind of man who could amass even a modest competence. He came to me in despair, and I paid all his debts. I felt that he could be useful to me in small but important ways — it was he who procured the bottles of peach brandy that my cyanide man liked to use.

When Simon Bolt told me that a meddling private investigator, Chloe McArthur, was starting to nose around Louis Gillette's affairs, I sent Charles Deacon after her to see where she went and what she did. He was partly successful in that, sending in a heavy to warn her and her associate off the case, but very soon, he began to show the kind of weakness and panic fear that had always been his chief failing. I knew that if two particular police detectives from Jubilee House were to lean on him much longer, he would crack, and start blabbing about me and my affairs.

I could not kill Deacon myself — we had shared too much history, and he was one of my own. My cyanide man did the deed. It upset me very much. I have made sure that Deacon's widow will never be in want.

Does my confession end here? Not quite yet. Soon, I'll pay my cyanide man handsomely to get rid of the restaurateur Goretti, who defied me, and insolently offered me a bottle of Lauretier Fils brandy as a 'present'. What did he mean by that? I won't wait to find out. So here my 'confession' stays until the demise of Goretti can be recorded in it. Then the whole manuscript will be consigned to the flames.

'Do we leave it here, Sergeant, until he's completed it?'

'Oh, no, Mr Fuller, he won't have a chance before we arrest him. We'll take this away with us, together with the holdall. Once we bring Tauber in, he'll produce a whole tribe of lawyers to fight his corner, I expect. We can handle it all very satisfactorily here, but the chief constable may want to bring in Scotland Yard.' He added, a little glumly, 'He usually does.'

* * *

Breakfast at the Savoy was always a meal to be savoured, eaten slowly, and received as something more than just breaking the fast of the night. The full English was delightful, the bacon in particular cooked to perfection. The toast was excellent, and the marmalade was served in an open dish, rather than in those little glass pots you got elsewhere.

His chauffeur would be here by eleven, parked right outside the hotel, and they would begin the leisurely journey back to Grace Hall. It was essential to maintain a facade of normality, one of the requisites of riding out any financial storm. And then when Goretti was disposed of, he'd begin a slow withdrawal from international finance, contenting himself with a more than modest fortune, enough for him and Corinne to live in the lap of luxury.

Corinne . . . What was she up to? Had she got wind of the trouble he'd found himself in? Perhaps. Well, one thing was certain, there would be no cyanide for Corinne! He'd find out who the handsome young man was and warn him off. They'd work something out.

A waiter approached.

'Excuse me, sir,' he said, 'but your chauffeur has arrived early. It will be quite all right for him to wait outside until you are ready to check out. He asked me to give you this envelope.'

It was a note from Williams.

Sir, the police have been here, and have removed items from the summer house. There was nothing we could do to stop them, and they would not tell me what those items were. I am ready here to take your orders.

What a senile fool he'd been! He had left a confession to murder where the police could find it, instead of locking it away somewhere safe.

He rang Williams at Grace Hall and told him to look in the drawer of the desk in the summer house, and tell him if there was a diary there. 'Kick down the door if necessary,' he said, 'but get in there and check.'

It seemed like an hour before Williams replied, but it was not as long as that. The door had been closed but unlocked, and the drawer was empty.

No more prevarications were possible: this was the end. There was only one course of action open to him, and he would take it.

* * *

The news broke the next morning, and the papers were full of the sensational disappearance of Manfred Tauber, the financier. Reporters had besieged the gates of Grace Hall, and scuffles had broken out between them and the Hall staff. The police had been called, and one of the staff, a man called Daniel O'Toole, had been arrested. One reporter had been taken to the Princess Diana Hospital with mild concussion. Mrs Tauber, too, seemed to have disappeared. Williams, the house manager (and some said the confidant) of Manfred Tauber was not available for comment.

'Police near to solving the mystery of the Arcade murder,' said the *Oldminster Gazette*. MR MONEYBAGS ON THE RUN, a headline in The *Sun* screamed. *Was absconding financier Tauber a killer?* asked the *Daily Mirror*. A studiously neutral voice on Radio 4 announced that the Oldshire Police were expected to make a full statement shortly. There would be a profile of Manfred Tauber following *The Archers*.

* * *

'It's only a matter of time, now, Sergeant, before we run him to ground.'

DI Glyn Edwards wasn't so sure.

'I agree, sir, that Tauber's condemned himself to life imprisonment by this confession. I expect the CPS have already started to prepare the indictments. But this is a man with a vast fortune who may well be able to buy a new identity for himself, and with greater success than his victim Louis Gillette did. He's bound to have money stashed away all over the world.'

DI French was sitting back in his chair, polishing his rimless glasses. It was the Monday following the search of Grace Hall.

'You may well be right, Glyn,' said DI French, 'but there are plenty of leads in that confession for us to follow up. Incidentally, the Met are more than willing to let you and me follow what leads we can find in London, so we'll not be treading on anyone's toes. We need to locate and interview this psychiatrist that Tauber consulted somewhere "off Harley Street". He may clam up, of course, probably will — patient confidentiality, and so forth. But it's a lead. Tauber says that he was starting to lose his self-confidence early this year and was beginning to feel that he was being spied upon. When we get him, his defence counsel will make much of that, and go for a plea of insanity.'

'He travels everywhere with a chauffeur, sir. That man could tell us where he went in London on Wednesday, and we could then interview whoever it was he went to see.'

'Yes, I was thinking that that would be something I'd like to do myself. I'll go out to Grace Hall this afternoon and see what I can get out of him.'

'According to his confession, Manfred Tauber is a mass killer. But only one murder — that of Louis Gillette — was committed recently. The three other murders we have been investigating were committed by the man whom he called "my cyanide man". If you're agreeable, I'd like to go hunting for him.'

'Yes, if that's what you want to do, Glyn. But where will you start?'

'Tauber mentions that man a lot in his confession, and more often than not he calls him "my man in the half-ruined hunting lodge". By trying to mask his identity he unwittingly tells us where the man is to be found.'

'And how will you locate this "half-ruined hunting lodge"?'

'For all his international connections Manfred Tauber is an Oldminster man, and I think his hired killer would live somewhere accessible to him in the county. I thought I'd visit the county surveyor in St Michael Street and see whether she knows of any properties in the area which had at one time been a hunting lodge, and were partly ruinous. It could be a listed building, and if it's a hunting lodge then it could be on the property of one of the big houses in the county, like Renfield Hall, or Billingford Chase, which is now the agricultural college. I've had a look online, but it's hard to narrow these things down just by searching for "hunting lodge".'

'Go down to St Michael Street now, Glyn, and see the surveyor. I'll get out to Grace Hall and see what I can find out from Tauber's chauffeur. And tomorrow, I'll see whether I can find that psychiatrist who treated Tauber in London.'

* * *

Detective Inspector French found Monkton, Manfred Tauber's chauffeur, polishing the Bentley on the forecourt of a range of garages that had at one time been a stable block. He was a man in his fifties, with one of those closed countenances that give nothing away. He showed neither alarm nor curiosity when French showed him his warrant card and asked him a question.

'I took Mr Tauber up to London on Wednesday, and we visited the Bank of England. After that, I drove him to the Stock Exchange, and then to the Ukrainian Embassy. We were going to visit New Court, the Rothschild's bank in St Swithin's Lane, but Mr Tauber changed his mind about that, and told me to take him to the Savoy.'

'What kind of mood was he in?'

'Mood? Well, he didn't seem very happy. I know nothing of my employer's business, I just drive him where he wants to go, and make sure he doesn't have to walk too far if we're parking in London.' A little wintry smile briefly crossed the chauffeur's face. 'Mr Tauber always appreciates me being able to park just about outside the door of wherever it is he wants to go. But he wasn't very happy that Wednesday.'

'Did he stay at the Savoy?'

'Yes. He said he'd stay the night. He told me to be ready and waiting for him at eleven o'clock Thursday morning.'

Monkton resumed his work of polishing the Bentley. He seemed to have lost interest in the proceedings. He had never thought to ask what was supposed to have happened to his employer if the police were looking for him.

'And did you?'

'Did I what?'

'Wait for him at eleven o'clock the next morning.'

'Yes, I did, but he wasn't there. And he'd left no message for me. So I came back here.'

'Now, I want you to think very carefully, Mr Monkton. Can you recall driving Mr Tauber to an address near Harley Street, in London? I'm speaking of earlier this year.'

'Harley Street?' The taciturn chauffeur showed a flicker of interest. 'Yes, I remember that. It was a long time ago, now. I think it was April. We stopped in Harley Street, and I assumed he was going to visit one of the doctors there. But he didn't. "Monkton," he said, "you stay here, and wait for me to return." That wasn't like him, so I watched where he went, and I saw him turn into Devonshire Street. I left the car and followed him to see where he went. He turned into Devonshire Mews and knocked on the door of number seventeen. I made a note of it and hared it back to the car.' Again, the little wintry smile. 'I wondered whether he was keeping a clandestine assignation. We went there a few times, later in the year, with me left sitting in the car in Harley Street, moving on and coming back again whenever the police came along.'

'You seem very knowledgeable about London, Mr Monkton.'

'That's because I'm a Londoner. I used to be a taxi driver years ago before I trained for chauffeur work, and that's why I know just about every street and alley in London.'

Talking so long to DI French seemed to have aroused his curiosity at last.

'Is the guvnor in some sort of trouble?' he asked. 'Apparently the police were swarming all over this place on Wednesday.'

'Well, we're just trying to find him in order to ask him a few questions. You've been a great help, Mr Monkton. Thank you very much.'

* * *

'Yes, Mr Edwards,' said the county surveyor. 'I think I know exactly where you'll find the "half-ruined hunting lodge". It was indeed one of four lodges bounding the Billingford Chase estate, as you'll see on this Ordnance Survey Map. It's about twelve miles out from Oldminster, on the B14, and since 1928, when the agricultural college took over the main house, it's been a private residence. There it is, see? It's practically invisible from the road because of the grove of oaks surrounding it. It's actually part of the village of Easton Peverell, which you can see here on the map. I say "village", but it's more of a hamlet, really.'

The county surveyor, an eager young woman with a neat bob and sporting a leather jacket, was only too anxious to help the police.

'Why is it described as half-ruined?' asked Glyn.

'Unlike many of these lodges, it was quite a substantial house, but a fire in 1943 left the back part of the building a ruin, and it was never rebuilt. The main part of the lodge was quite unaffected by the fire, and is quite a nice little property, so I'm told. There was some talk by the local historical society of applying for listed status — it was built in 1830 — but nothing came of it.'

'And do you know who's living there now?'

'I don't, I'm afraid. But you'll be able to find out by consulting the electoral rolls at the Town Hall.'

* * *

DS Edwards drove out to Easton Peverell the next morning. The lodge was just as the surveyor had described, quite a substantial house with a stuccoed frontage, with an ivy-covered ruin at the back. The area was densely wooded, though Glyn could see some of the houses of the hamlet at the end of the main road.

He had looked up the new tenant in the electoral rolls and found that his name was Stephen Holroyd. The 'half-ruined hunting lodge' was known officially as Billingford South Lodge. Mr Holroyd, a comfortable-looking man wearing jeans and a T-shirt, was pottering about in the small front garden. He seemed very pleased to see Glyn and invited him into the lodge.

It was a rather gloomy place, as the windows were small and the only view from them was of tangled overgrown bushes, but there was nothing gloomy about Mr Holroyd.

'Sit here, by the fire, Sergeant Edwards,' he said. 'It's a fair drive out from town to Easton. What can I do for you? Would you like some tea? Well, it's as you wish.'

'I'd like you to tell me something about the lessee of this lodge, the man you're renting it from for six months. I saw from the records that his name is Clifford Stott.'

'This is about the cyanide murders, isn't it? I never thought I'd be mixed up in anything as exciting as that. I retired from teaching in the summer, and as I've no family, I thought I'd like to live out in the country for a while, to recharge my batteries. I lived most of my life in Chichester, but I wanted a change, and when I saw this place on offer for rent, with a little photograph — it was in the window of Morphett's, the stationers in Chichester, I knew it would suit me. Do you know it? Morphett's, I mean. Anyway, I came out here on the bus — well, three buses really. I don't drive a car. Never got round to it, somehow! Anyway, there it is.'

Mr Holroyd had talked himself to a standstill. He was an agreeable, red-faced man with thinning grey hair, and bright blue eyes under bushy eyebrows. Glyn thought, *I bet he taught woodwork.*

'What was he like, this Clifford Stott? We think he might be able to help us over these cyanide murders. I can't tell you more that, Mr Holroyd.'

'Isn't it exciting? You don't get much excitement teaching woodwork, apart from the occasional confrontation between some little boy and a sharp chisel! What was he like? Well, he was what I'd call a mousy little man, not very well built, but strong, I think. A man with plenty of nervous energy. He was about five foot ten.'

'Did he have any outstanding characteristics?'

'Well, no, he didn't. He just looked like everybody else, if you know what I mean. He'd never stand out in a crowd. He wore glasses, just ordinary bog-standard ones, nothing fancy. Oh, and his fingers were stained with what I think must have been acid. We had a chemistry teacher like that, where I worked. His fingers used to get stained with acid — one of the perks of the job, he used to say!'

'Did he say what he did for a living?'

'Yes. He told me that he was a chemist, and when I asked him whether he worked for Boots, he said no, not that kind of chemist, but an industrial chemist who used to work in a laboratory in some big chemical concern or other. It's no good asking me because I can't remember. "What you call a chemist," he said, "we call a pharmacist." Very insistent on that, he was.'

Glyn listened to all this with growing excitement. This Clifford Stott, the man who didn't stand out in a crowd, was Manfred Tauber's hired assassin. He had his name, and his profession, now he needed to find out where he was lying low.

'No, Sergeant, he never said where he was going. I asked him out of politeness, but he just laughed the matter off. "I may not come back at all, Mr Holroyd," he said. "Maybe I'll retire too, like you, and go on my travels!" Yes, he wasn't a very big fellow, but I rather liked him. Harmless sort of chap, I thought.'

'And you paid him six months' rent in advance?'

'I did. I paid him in cash, which pleased him greatly. I remember he shook hands with me, and said it was a pleasure to do business with me.'

So, no bank details, which could have been used to track him down. He'd consult Mr French and ask whether they could leak a little story about Mr Clifford Stott to the *Oldminster Gazette*. The man's history didn't matter at this stage. The thing to do now was to run him to ground.

'Are any of Stott's things still here?'

'No, it was unfurnished. Everything you see here is mine. You know, Sergeant, if Mr Stott was connected with those cyanide murders, maybe he's done a bunk — maybe he never intended to come back here. That big financier who's scarpered — it was all over the paper. They're saying that he was the man behind those murders. So maybe Stott was his hatchet man!'

* * *

'It's most irregular, Inspector French,' said the psychiatrist, who practised in a suite of musty rooms on the first floor of 17 Devonshire Mews, 'it's most irregular to discuss a patient's details without his written consent. Patient confidentiality, like the confessional, is sacrosanct.'

'All I want to know, sir,' said DI French, 'is whether Mr Tauber consulted you in a professional capacity on several occasions earlier in the year. I think you will know that your client seems to have absconded, and that we have very good reason to believe that he has been directly involved in a number of particularly cruel murders.'

He paused, to let the import of his words sink in. The psychiatrist had said what he was obliged to say, but he did not look like a pompous man, who would climb upon his professional high horse. The psychiatrist sighed, and motioned to a chair.

'Sit down, Mr French. I want to tell you about a certain type of patient that I get here. I'm not talking about any named patient, you understand.'

He looked fixedly at French for a moment and was evidently satisfied at the look of understanding that French gave him. No names, no pack drill.

'The condition underlying this type of patient's dilemma, Mr French, is an inability to feel guilt, and it is this inability that prevents him from moving forward out of his particular psychosis. Such patients will readily confess to actions that are clearly reprehensible, and then bemoan the fact that they can't feel guilty about them. They want to regret these deeds, but can't. They are impelled at all times by self-interest, and the instinct for self-preservation.'

'So, people of that kind are pure villain, with nothing to redeem them?'

'Not entirely. One can often draw out the better side of their nature, their philanthropy, remarkable acts of kindness, and sudden, often rash fits of generosity. But then, the dark side of their nature intrudes, and we would once again come back to this inability to feel guilt.'

'You are talking about psychopaths?'

'And narcissists, too. Nowadays we have lots of different ways of describing such symptoms — some personality disorders blend into others. You see, there is no black and white in psychiatry. All human beings are complex creations — I don't mean that in the biological or theological sense. I mean that we are all partly responsible for creating ourselves through the choices we make, and the masks that we feel compelled to assume. I hope what I have described will be of some use to you.'

14. A TOAST TO THE FUTURE

In the empty back bar of a little pub which stood on the edge of an obscure bay on the Kerry Coast, Manfred Tauber sat deep in thought. A copy of last week's *Irish Independent* lay on the table, and he had been reading its account of the absconding financier who had left a trail of ruin behind him.

Well, it was true, as far as it went. His British and European paper empires had collapsed, and there were warrants out for his arrest. But there was more to the world than Britain and Europe, and for years he had quietly built up a very decent dollar fortune which he had deposited in one of the many private banks to be found in Guatemala City, banks which, while minding your business for you, minded their own, as well.

True, Guatemala had an extradition treaty with the UK, but what of that? The country had had a turbulent history of coups and counter-coups, of doubtful alliances with foreign powers, but it continued to survive even the stranglehold of the South American drug cartels. And its judiciary had a reputation for being deeply corrupt, which could prove helpful.

When he had been alerted by Williams that the police had raided Grace Hall, he had left the Savoy immediately, and boarded one of the many daily flights to Dublin from

Heathrow. A private-hire car had driven him along the wearisome route to the little bay on the Kerry Coast, where he had been received by Mike Ahearn, the proprietor of Michael's Bar, a man who also catered for anyone who wanted to stay out of sight for a while in what was one of the most obscure and sparsely populated places on the west coast. You could hole up there, drink Mike's real ale, and be served food that actually had some flavour.

For the purposes of his flight, he was now calling himself 'Mr Smith', but Mike Ahearn knew who he was. He and Michael Ahearn went back a long way.

Ahearn came into the back room, and stood, arms folded, looking at his paying guest. Mike was a big, ginger-headed man with tattooed arms and an earring in his right ear.

'It'll be tomorrow, then, Mr Smith, the thirtieth, as arranged,' he said. 'A little motorboat will take you from here to a yacht standing a mile out of the bay, and the yacht will take you to the Guatemalan cargo ship *Rosario*, which will be riding at anchor in the Atlantic shipping lanes.' He reached into a pocket and brought out a paper wallet. 'All the paperwork's in there.'

'You've been very kind, Mike,' said Mr Smith, 'very helpful. I don't suppose I'll be coming here again. I'll miss you.'

'Likewise, Mr Smith. You've always been more than generous when you've asked me to arrange this kind of thing for you, but this time — ten grand! I'll have some lunch ready for you at one o'clock.'

When Ahearn had gone, Manfred Tauber sat very still, thinking. His fortnight's stay in County Kerry had done much to clear his head and banish the phantom of Louis Gillette. It had also given him and Mike Ahern time to set things in motion. He had long ago purchased a villa in one of the tourist centres of Guatemala and had installed a complete household of servants who had nothing to do, year after year, but dust the furniture and tend to the grounds. When he was settled in, he'd send for Corinne, and she would join him there.

At least, he assumed that she would. Corinne knew that he was 'shady', but she knew nothing of his business, or of his secret Guatemalan retreat. Would she come? Or would she look elsewhere for consolation? Well, it didn't matter. Whatever she did, he would see that she was all right.

He would miss playing the squire at Grace Hall — any creditors in the UK would swoop down on it for reparation. Well, not many men in their seventies were able to start an entirely new life, as he was about to do. But he'd miss his old friend and former partner Simon Bolt. Perhaps they would meet again, some time. Though Simon had never had much of a penchant for skulduggery.

He had long ago transferred ownership of the cemetery at Grace Hall to a private trust. Magda would continue to rest in peace, and one day he would join her there.

The door of the back room opened, and Clifford Stott came in. At first, Tauber thought it was an apparition, like those visions of Louis Gillette that had plagued him since his death. But no, it was his cyanide man in the flesh, even down to a bottle wrapped in tissue paper in his hand. He was wearing a green tweed three-piece suit, a plaid shirt and a bow tie. He looked like an advertisement for gents' tailoring in a fifties magazine.

A cold fear began to settle on Manfred Tauber's heart. How had Stott found him, and run him to ground, here, in one of the remotest corners of Western Ireland?

'You don't look very happy to see me, Mr Tauber,' said Stott, smiling. 'Or are you just surprised? I suppose you thought I acted alone all these years whenever you asked me to oblige you? But no, I had my own little network of "spies", if that's not too dramatic a word to use, and after our last — er — contract, I had one of my fellows watch what you did. There's only six of them, but they're all skilled in what they do. One of them followed you here, all the way from the Savoy to this remote spot, so when I knew where you'd holed up, I came to say goodbye to you.'

Clifford Stott placed the bottle on the table.

'You know, Mr Tauber, I always prided myself on my anonymity, and I was very vexed when I found my name mentioned in the papers as someone who the police were anxious to interview. Very vexed indeed. You didn't tell them, did you?'

'Me? Don't be ridiculous! Why should I tell anybody that I was on intimate terms with a professional killer? No, it was one or other of those two policemen, I expect. I never underestimated either of them. DI French and DS Edwards. So, what are you going to do, Mr Stott?'

'Well, I've managed to remain incognito in a B & B up in Cumbria, out of harm's way, but I have plans to go somewhere quite different, somewhere where nobody will be able to find me. A place where "true joys are to be found", so to speak. So, I've come to say goodbye. And I thought it would be a good idea if we shared a last drink together before we each go our separate ways. For old time's sake, you know.'

Stott removed the tissue paper from the bottle, and Tauber saw that it was a bottle of Lauretier Fils Peach Brandy. Should he call for help? A word from him and Mike Ahearn would come in and teach Stott a lesson he'd never forget.

'You have a peculiar sense of humour, Mr Stott,' he said. 'Nothing would persuade me to drink what must be the most fatal brandy in the world.'

Clifford Stott laughed.

'I take your point, Mr Tauber,' he said, 'and perhaps it wasn't the most tasteful thing for me to do. But we've both been so bound up with this brandy that it seemed only right for us to use it to drink a toast to our successful futures.'

'What did you do to that accountant, Edmund Salis?'

'I broke into his house and found a liquid medicine prescribed for him to take every day. The stuff smelled foul anyway — I expect he didn't even notice the smell of the cyanide I replaced it with.'

'And Deacon?'

'Poor Mr Deacon! His wife was never out of the house, so I met him on his way back from the pub and persuaded him to come and sit with me in the local park to share a drink — two old sots together. When he saw the bottle of peach brandy he sobered up, all right. He was quite adamant, in a feebly blustering sort of way, that he would not drink his glass of brandy. So I seized him by the throat, half throttled him, and poured it down his gullet. I didn't intend to leave him in the pond, but he fell into it in his death throes. Better to leave him there than scrabble about trying to retrieve him, I thought. Plus, it would send out a strong signal to those awkward clients of yours to toe the line — or else!'

'It was certainly effective,' said Tauber. 'But I didn't like it. Poor fellow!'

There was a dresser in the back room, with an array of glasses on display. Stott brought two bulbous brandy glasses over to the table, unscrewed the bottle, and filled them almost to the brim. Tauber thought, *Is Stott on the level? Has he really come all this way just to bid me a fond farewell?*

Evidently Clifford Stott had read his mind, because once again he laughed, and raised his glass.

'No prussic acid this time, Mr Tauber!' he said. 'Here's to our joint futures!'

He drained the glass and put it back on the table. Manfred Tauber did the same. They had indeed been partners in crime, and it seemed that they were to part as friends.

Clifford Stott began to talk. He betrayed no curiosity about Tauber's plan to start a new life. Instead, he began to talk about his own early life, his interest in chemistry, and his work for a large industrial concern. Manfred Tauber thought how banal and boring it was. He stifled a yawn, and then closed his eyes. He could still hear Clifford Stott droning on.

When Mike Ahearn came in at one o'clock, he found Manfred Tauber and Clifford Stott still sitting at the table, with their heads cradled in their arms, with two empty brandy glasses and a bottle on the table beside them. They were both dead.

* * *

DI French and DS Edwards arrived at the Garda Headquarters in Dublin's Phoenix Park the day after the bodies of Manfred Tauber and Clifford Stott had been discovered by Mike Ahearn. They were sitting in one of the laboratories of Forensic Science Ireland, listening to Dr Seamus O'Connell, one of the department's experts on criminal poisoning.

'They both died from the ingestion of coniine,' he said. 'It's an alkaloid derived from hemlock, *Conium maculatum*. I gather that Stott was himself a trained chemist and had used doctored brandy for sinister purposes before this.'

'What do you think happened in that room, Doctor?' asked DI French.

'Well, I'd say it was murder and suicide. Stott brought that bottle of brandy laced with coniine, and perhaps to allay the other man's fear, drank his glass straight away. His companion then did the same. They would have both gone quietly to sleep. Death would have supervened within half an hour.'

'Years ago,' said DS Edwards, 'they used to say that people like that had "cheated the gallows". But I don't know. They were both killers, and they topped each other.'

'The smooth-talking Tauber had an escape route all planned out,' said DI French. 'That man Ahearn told the Garda all about it.'

'Did all those murders get to Clifford Stott in the end?' wondered Glyn Edwards. 'Perhaps he decided to make some kind of atonement for it by committing suicide, but not before he'd carried out his last murder, that of his patron Manfred Tauber. They could accompany each other on their journey to — well, to wherever it is they're going. The world's well rid of them.'

'I suppose we should be glad of the outcome,' said DI French when he and Glyn Edwards had taken their seat in the London plane, 'but it hasn't been a satisfactory case to my way of thinking. We went after Louis Gillette's killer, but without Manfred Tauber's written confession, I don't think we would have solved that murder at all. We stumbled on things, Glyn, rather than uncovering them by careful police work. Still, both killers are dead, and as you said, the world's well rid of them.'

'I saw Jack Prosser last week,' said Glyn. 'He avoided a custodial sentence but was fined one thousand pounds for disturbing a corpse. I think he was very lucky — I'd have locked him up. He's emigrating to New Zealand, so Mrs Gillette will no longer go in fear of him trying to rekindle their affair. He seemed to have got a grip of himself, and faced up to reality, but even as I was talking to him, I could see him in my mind's eye attacking Gillette's dead body with that statuette. I wished him well and left. But I didn't shake hands with him.'

* * *

Just after Christmas, Chloe McArthur met Corinne Tauber in the King's Arcade. Chloe had gone there to buy a book on Thai cooking from Fox's Bookshop at number 18. Corinne had been to Stoddard's the jewellers, where she had received a very good price for the diamond ring that Manfred had insisted on buying for her.

Corinne seemed to be in very good spirits and invited Chloe to join her for coffee in Maison Jacques' Patisserie at number 3. She was as beautiful as ever, exquisitely dressed, and with not a hair out of place.

'Poor Manfred was always making me buy things, Chloe,' she said. 'He was ever so sweet! Of course, I had to move out of Grace Hall when it was seized by the creditors, but I have a very nice flat in Mayfair, and Victor's got this marvellous house in the country. You've seen Victor? He's ever so handsome, and so very romantic. I'm sure we'll get on very well together. I suppose I should marry him, but it's a bit early, with poor Manfred being dead only a month.'

'I'm glad to see you looking so well,' said Chloe. Common sense told her that she shouldn't like this gold digger, but she couldn't help it: Corinne was good company, a raiser of spirits.

'I wasn't at Manfred's funeral,' said Chloe. 'I suppose it was a quiet affair?'

'Well, you see, Manfred left instructions that he was to be buried with his first wife in the mausoleum in the grounds of Grace Hall. But I thought that would be too dreary, my dear, so I had him cremated, and the ashes scattered on the rose garden at the crematorium. I think that in the end that's what Manfred would have liked. Don't you agree?'

No, thought Chloe, *I don't agree. Really, Corinne, you are the limit!*

'I shan't stay in Oldminster,' said Corinne. 'I much prefer London. And anyway, it's not very nice for me, knowing that Manfred murdered Lydia's husband. What could I say, if I met her? "I'm awfully sorry, Lydia". It's not enough. So I'm moving to London for good at the end of the month. I'm just down this weekend to see to one or two things.'

Corinne gave Chloe McArthur a rueful smile.

'All the servants went as soon as the truth about poor Manfred came out,' she said. 'Williams was snapped up by some tycoon or other who's building himself a ghastly modern mansion somewhere in Oxfordshire. And our wonderful chauffeur, Monkton, has got himself a very nice position with one of those London private bankers. So everything's turned out for the best, I suppose.'

The two women left the café, and by some kind of unspoken consent walked up towards the Rembrandt Gallery.

'Oh, look!' cried Chloe. 'The optician's has moved to number five, which was vacant. And there are workmen in their old shop, knocking it into the Rembrandt Gallery.' Evidently Lydia was expanding the premises. She had told Chloe all about her old friend Rupert Danecourt, and his plans for the gallery. The four adjacent shops were full of workmen, shopfitters, painters, plumbers — a continuous blaze of light and hive of activity. Posters in the windows proclaimed:

The New Rembrandt Gallery. Grand Opening on New Year's Day by His Worship the Lord Mayor.

Chloe and Corinne left the Arcade and walked down to the car park by the Town Hall. Chloe got into her little Citroen. Corinne made her way to a very expensive-looking Lexus, where she was greeted by the incredibly handsome man called Victor. Was he a wealthy man? Or was he another gold digger, who thought that Corinne was a wealthy widow? Well, time would tell.

She told Noel Greenspan of her encounter when she returned to the office.

'Corinne's not a bad sort,' he said, 'and she really is a stunner. Incidentally, I've looked into that Victor of hers. A little private investigation, you know. He started life as a model, but then moved into the car business. He has quite a big franchise in London. So yes, worth a few bob. Our Corinne won't go short of anything.

'Incidentally, Lance Middleton's gone to stay with that lawyer friend of his in Paris, so he'll be able to indulge his gourmet's taste to his heart's content. I think that battering he got in Newcastle took it out of him more than he realised. He's going to stay there until spring, a kind of prolonged convalescence.'

'Do you think it's put him off working for us in the future?'

'Certainly not. He can always be lured down here by one of your mesmerising meals, and in any case he's too full of curiosity to resist a call to arms!

'Now, I've just had a man in here who's the victim of a poison-pen letter writer, accusing him of murder, embezzlement, and more besides. I told him we'd investigate. He gave me all the letters to look at. They were all posted from Goose-pen Street Post Office. So come on, Mrs McArthur, let's get to work!'

* * *

Lydia Gillette and Rupert Danecourt walked together from All Saints churchyard, where they had laid a garland of winter blooms on Louis Gillette's grave. It was a bright, cold winter's day.

Danecourt had become a frequent visitor to Gladstone Road and had grown to be very fond of the pleasant Victorian suburb of North End. Whenever he visited, he and Lydia would always contrive to take a leisurely walk along the treelined roads, usually ending up at Clarence Park, a sort of communal garden with playing fields, though today, they had chosen once more to visit Louis Gillette's grave.

They came back to Lydia's house, where a cheerful fire was still burning in the drawing-room grate. Lydia made them a pot of coffee, and they settled down on one of the big oatmeal settees.

'What about the footfall?' asked Rupert, and Lydia knew what he meant.

'I'd say it's increased a hundredfold. I never imagined that the gallery would be the instant success that it's proved to be. It's always crowded, and we seem to be providing the kind of service that people want. The café side of the business has proved to be a great success.'

'What does your father think?'

'He's delighted with it all. Oh, and he had the sense not to interfere with the funding. The bank loan will be paid off from our profits, as you suggested, though I must admit that it's reassuring to know that Daddy's still there! I feel — oh, I feel as though I've come to life again!'

'Has he tried to lure you back to London? You told me that after Louis's death he was constantly badgering you to leave Oldminster, and there was a time when you were about to give in to him.'

'No, Rupert, he knows that I belong here. As to this house . . .'

She looked around the room, with its neutral décor, and its high ceilings, and suddenly realised that she rather liked it. She saw Rupert watching her and realised that he was reading her thoughts.

'This is a very nice house, Lydia,' he said. 'All it needs is a good firm of interior designers to come in and give it a makeover. Oh, and a good landscape firm to see to the grounds, which have great potential. If the back lawn was properly revived, you could hold summer receptions there in a decent marquee — garden parties, you know, in aid of local charities, but tied in with the gallery . . . You could have samples of the latest acquisitions on show . . . Oh, and raffles, you know, perhaps in conjunction with that nice woman in the bookshop, with books as prizes. That would give her some free publicity. What was her name? Eleanor Fox. She lives near here, doesn't she, in Palmerston Road.'

Lydia Gillette burst out laughing.

'You're doing it again! You're planning out my life for me — showing me things I hadn't noticed before! I'm glad you like my house.'

'I like it very much,' said Rupert Danecourt. 'I'd like to live here. In Oldminster, I mean, and in this house in particular. I've no special attachment to Uckfield.'

Lydia Gillette heard what her friend had as yet left unspoken. It was a curious, quirky proposal, but a proposal nonetheless.

'Will you give me time, Rupert? Louis's not three months dead. But when you first called here last year, and we went to see Louis's grave, I felt some kind of force or spirit urging me not to let you go. So yes, towards the end of the year — maybe earlier — we'll do what you've left unspoken, and call on the vicar at All Saints.'

Rupert and Lydia sat there by the fire, discussing business, recounting episodes in their past lives, conditionally defining what would be their future together until it was time for Rupert to catch his train back to Uckfield, and for Lydia to start living her life to the full once more, knowing in her heart that Louis had forgiven her.

THE END

ALSO BY NORMAN RUSSELL

THE OLDMINSTER MYSTERIES
Book 1: AN INVITATION TO MURDER
Book 2: AN ANTIQUE MURDER
Book 3: THE SECRET OF BAGNETT HALL
Book 4: NO CHOICE BUT MURDER

Thank you for reading this book.

If you enjoyed it please leave feedback on Amazon or Goodreads, and if there is anything we missed or you have a question about, then please get in touch. We appreciate you choosing our book.

Founded in 2014 in Shoreditch, London, we at Joffe Books pride ourselves on our history of innovative publishing. We were thrilled to be shortlisted for Independent Publisher of the Year at the British Book Awards.

www.joffebooks.com

We're very grateful to eagle-eyed readers who take the time to contact us. Please send any errors you find to corrections@joffebooks.com. We'll get them fixed ASAP.